BUYING TIRAN

HISSA WARRIOR
BOOK 2

DISCLAIMER

This is a work of fiction. Names, characters, businesses, places, events and incidents are either the products of the author's imagination or used in a fictitious manner. Any resemblance to actual persons, living or dead, or actual events is purely coincidental.

All rights reserved:

No part of this book may be reproduced or transmitted in any form or by any means, electronic or mechanical, including photocopying, recording, or by any information storage and retrieval system, without prior permission in writing from the author.

Translation:

Don't steal the stories I worked so hard on, and occasionally cried over. Don't get upset at the absolutely made-up story lines: this is a romance, so of course it isn't realistic, duh! Don't be petty and hate on it because it isn't not your kink. We've all got different tastes and there's no shame in that.

Warning: Author is dyslexic as hell.

Feel free to contact me with questions, requests, or comments:

Author@RK-Munin.com

Pick up some free novella by signing up for my newsletter. You can find the sign-up links on my website:

www.rk-munin.com

And, as with many writers, your reviews on Amazon, Goodreads, and/or Kindle help immeasurably, even if it's just clicking on the stars.

Thank you to all my readers!

CONTENT WARNING

-Slavery is witnessed and talked about.
-Sexual assault is mentioned.
-There are scenes of violence and battle.
-For a portion of a chapter where the FMC is unable to move or talk but is still aware of what is going on around her.

DEDICATION

Thanks Kirsten P. for all the help! You're not just family, you're a valued friend too.

CHAPTER

1

Mara Lost, Captain of the Witch, an independent freight hauler, frowns as she searches the small stage in front of her. There are three women and two men standing there naked except for the obedience collars around their necks. One of the men wears a dead expression, the kind someone has when they're just waiting to die. The three females are doing their best to be seductive, hoping to be bought by a single owner instead of a collective where their bodies will be shared and bartered among the members.

But there's only one figure on the stage that draws Mara's attention. The second male, towering over his fellow slaves, doesn't look seductive or emotionally frozen, he looks furious. He glares at the crowd as they bid on the woman in front of him, promising violence to anyone who tries to do anything to him he doesn't want.

"Excuse me, are you a human female?" a small furry creature called a Fozin asks her with a tug on the sleeve of her biosuit. She can tell this Fozin is male because of the bright color of his fur. Fozins are traders and, more often than not, swindlers as well. Anyone making deals with the Fozin needs to be extra careful or risk getting gouged at best, defrauded at worst.

She regards the little alien with a show of teeth, so it steps back and waves its three-fingered paw in apology. "Amends. I meant no disrespect," he chirps out quickly. "But I've never seen one of you before, and my young were curious." He indicates behind him, and Mara looks over to see a female Fozin with two young standing on either side of her. Mara gives a little sigh. This isn't an uncommon occurrence for her in this area of the galaxy where humans are few and far between. Her rarity makes for many propositions and a number of annoying encounters when individuals won't accept "NO" for an answer.

"Yes, I'm a human and female. Go tell your young so they know not to approach us without invitation. Humans are dangerous and quick to anger."

The Fozin chitters with amusement at her words, showing the single long fang at the very front of his mouth. Fozin might look small and harmless, but that fang contains a neurotoxin deadly enough to kill within seconds. They also have little spikes under the skin at the back of their hand containing the same toxin. There are only a few species out there that aren't susceptible to their neurotoxin, so despite their size, no one tends to bully or abuse them.

The Fozin standing in front of her laughing is yet another example of how unfair the universe is.

Unlike most species out there, humans are generally seen as relatively harmless, lacking claws, fangs, poison, or much in the way of size compared to others. But Mara figures maybe she can spread some rumors and create a little fear of humans among those who've never met one. Occasionally she's successful, but apparently not this time.

"Go away," she commands and turns her attention back to the stage, but the little Fozin stays and tugs on her sleeve again.

"I know of one who wants humans," he tells her. "I

could broker a deal. You would come away very wealthy."

Mara glares at him. "You really think I'm willing to sell myself into slavery? You're an idiot and a bad negotiator."

The small creature stiffens and pulls back his upper lip to show his displeasure at her words. There's no greater insult to a Fozin than to ridicule their bargaining skills.

The Fozin's hair stands up on end, an unconscious instinct in the species to make them look just a little bigger. His movements are jerky when he tugs on her sleeve again. "You misunderstand human, but I'm sure that's common with your kind. The offer is for contracted servitude with a termination clause. And you've not even heard the price. The credits are very good."

"Go. Away. Now." She enunciates each word and makes a shooing motion with her hands. The Fozin's fur ripples, a sign of frustration, and his single fang twitches a little.

"Watch your auction and do your business. We'll discuss this when you are in a more rational frame of mind, female," he declares and tosses a small data card at her. Without seeing if she catches it, he turns and walks away.

She grabs it out of the air before it can hit her in the face. The data card is a standard information holder. If she presses in the center, his image would pop up with his name, location, profession, and all the ways to contact him. All she would need to do is press it into any nearby communication center, and it would contact him.

She tosses it into a nearby trash receptacle with a shake of her head. She's sure she hasn't seen the last of that Fozin. She wonders if she should've played along a little to find out who the buyer is. It's generally a good idea to know who's interested in spending good money to interact with humans because they might have interacted with her sister at some point, however unlikely it might be.

Most who offer to spend time with her only want to see what it's like. They don't want to bother with the expense of keeping a human as a full-time slave, especially in this solar system. Large and sturdy agricultural workers are in demand, not weak humans. Slaves around here need to be able to earn their keep. Even if they're bought for sex, they're expected to work in other ways also.

She'll make sure to string the Fozin along next time so she can get more information. For now, she has other pressing matters. She turns her attention back to the auction taking place in front of her.

She can't see her sister on the stage so she should just leave and take her ship, Witch, to the next assignment. But she can't make herself turn away. She stands there watching the large male in the back, scowling at everyone around him. He's much taller than her five foot nine inches, with broad shoulders and a muscular chest. The smaller slave in front of him keeps her from seeing much below his pectoral muscles, but she's sure everything down there is equally muscled and magnificent.

She's surprised to find she can't take her eyes off him. She hates these slave markets and normally leaves the moment she confirms her sister isn't there. Not today. Today she stands captivated by the striking male who's obviously new to slavery.

"Sold!" The auctioneer shouts and one of the more beautiful women in the front delicately picks her way off the small stage. A beaming man presents a clerk with his data bracelet and Mara can hear the beeping of the financial transaction. The woman looks happy. She should. She's been bought by an individual. And by the look of the small, portly, eager man, he'll be easy to wrap around her finger. It's the best scenario a slave like her can hope for.

The moment the woman is off the stage, the auctioneer starts up again. "This female might not be as stunning as our tall beauty from before, but I've been told she has training. If you want to know more about that training, you're going to need to buy her first!" The audience obediently chuckles, and the bidding starts.

Mara hears the large engines of the space station fire up to keep the massive structure in a stable orbit around the nearby planet. The station's not particularly well-kept so the grated metal floor under her feet vibrates violently for a moment before settling. There are a few gasps as people are knocked off balance and others reach out to nearby surfaces to steady themselves. Familiar with the old station's issues, the announcer stops the bidding until the station settles and everyone regains their feet.

Due to her training, Mara doesn't suffer a moment of unsteadiness and doesn't need to grab anything to keep her balance either. She notices the large man also shifts easily with the motion of the station under his feet. She wonders if he's a trained fighter too or perhaps just experienced with badly programmed orbital stability systems.

Suddenly he looks up and catches her eye. Her heartbeat increases, and she feels a shock go through her as if she's touched a live wire. Now focusing on her, his scowl deepens, and she almost takes a step back.

He's a slave, shackled with an obedience collar, she reminds herself. *He can't hurt me.*

At the same time, she feels vaguely threatened by the large male. Then a sense of sadness hits her.

Despite his attractiveness, he definitely won't be used for sex. He might be beautiful and sculpted, but he's also fierce and frightening. He'll probably be shipped down to the planet for agricultural work. He'll be half-starved and beaten to keep him in line. Without a doubt, he'll be dead within several months.

She knows in her heart he'll die because he'll try to escape. He'll make the attempt over and over and over again until his owners decide he isn't worth the effort and have him "put down."

For no reason Mara can explain, her eyes fill with tears at the thought. When the last slave in front of him is sold and he stands alone on the platform, she can't help the small gasp that escapes her once she has an unobstructed view.

To put it bluntly, he has a sublime body. The guard behind him nudges him forward with a shock stick and the man turns and actually roars. The sound echoes off the walls, causing the buzzing audience to fall silent. Mara watches the man flash sharp fangs, making the guard flinch.

The man looks back at the audience and searches until he finds her eyes again. She walks a step or two forward but stops the moment their eyes meet. He gives her a low snarl, showing off those sharp canines.

"Well, we've got a lively one here," the auctioneer declares with forced jocularity. "Who would like to start the bidding at 50 credits?"

Not a single person raises their hand.

"Is it one of those hybrids?" someone whispers to the person next to them.

"No, he's Hissa," the other person answers. "I don't know if we've ever had one at auction before."

Ah, Mara thinks, *that explains it.*

Hissa are an alien species almost wiped out by disease decades ago. That's pretty much all she knows about them, except the location of their home solar system. Mara never expected to see one, considering they tend to stick to their own territory.

How did this one end up at a slave auction? A deep

biting anger fills her. She firmly believes slavery should be outlawed throughout the universe. But being a slave seems doubly worse for this proud male. The person or collective that buys him will think they've gotten a bargain, but he'll turn out to be more trouble than he's worth. His spirit will never be broken, so his life would end far too soon. His body will be tossed in a pit somewhere, along with colony refuse. His people will never know what happened to him.

"20 credits."

Everyone looks over at Mara, and she realizes she's the one who called out. What is she doing? Twenty credits are almost everything she has!

"I have 20," the announcer says with a flourish of his hand. "Is anyone interested in going to 25?"

No one raises a hand. No one moves.

"Maybe 23?" The announcer tries one more time. The slave gives another roar as the guard behind him tries to push him forward again, and the entire audience, except for Mara, takes a step back.

"Very well, Number 323 is sold for 20 credits."

Mara feels stunned. She's done it. She's bought herself a slave. She feels sick to her stomach. What's she going to do with a slave? The clerk is suddenly at her side demanding she show him her data bracelet to pay for her purchase. She takes her eyes off the man to look at the bossy clerk and runs her bracelet against his small device. He presents her with a data pad, and she puts her thumb on the pad to complete the transaction.

"You're suicidal," the clerk mutters as he presents her with a small data card with a copy of the transaction on it. The data card is proof of her ownership and allows her to sell or transfer the slave like any other property. Then he hands her the small black fob that can open, lock, or reset the obedience collar around her slave's neck to her voice. She tucks everything into one of her biosuit pockets with a shaking hand.

The clerk gives the large male one more quick look and pales a little. "I'd key his obedience collar to your voice right away," he tells her, then scurries off.

Suddenly the giant is in front of her, his wide shoulders blocking out everything behind him. Most of him is a light green color except for his head. Starting at a point between his eyes, the scale pattern V's out until it covers the top of his head. Those scales were black up on the stage, but now that he's standing in front of her, staring down at her intensely, it's turned a deep, eggplant purple.

Up close she can see his ears are almost non-existent, just tiny flaps around ear holes in the side of his head. His eyes are beautiful, with hourglass-shaped pupils surrounded by a purple so bright his eyes appear to glow on their own.

His teeth are even larger than she thought, especially those pronounced canines. Adding to his deadly appearance, his hands are large and tipped with black claw-like nails. His species has four fingers, all of them the same length, but like humans, only one of them is an opposable digit.

On top of having intimidating teeth and claws, her purchase isn't smiling or looking at her for guidance. He's not relaxed or subservient. He stands there, shoulders back, head held proud, nostrils flaring as he breathes deeply. He's not shy about getting close and towering over her. Then three hundred pounds of angry male peels back his lips and gives a low growl.

Yup, she thinks grimly, *I'm a soft-hearted idiot.*

CHAPTER 2

"Sold!"

That's all Tiran hears. He's been sold. Someone just bought him. He's property.

How did this happen? Where is the rest of his team? The last thing he remembers is settling down in the sleep pod; then he's abruptly wakened with shouting and shock sticks. A day later they strip him of his clothes and force him out onto this stage.

He stumbled forward with the other slaves, enraged and ready to kill whoever tried to buy him. He watched the others get sold and waited for his turn; then he saw her. She stood so still and silent in the crowd. She didn't shout or jeer as the other slaves were sold. She frowned and looked sad. Tiran had the strongest urge to go to her and comfort her. He couldn't take his eyes off her.

But now she owns him. He hopes he doesn't need to kill her to gain his freedom.

The guard is bringing up the shock stick again, expecting him to fight and resist. Instead, he moves forward with swift, easy grace and jumps off the small stage. The crowd parts in front of him as he makes his way to the woman who bought him.

She's small by his standards. Although he only has vague memories of Hissa women, he can clearly remember his mother standing even with his father. He remembers her easily picking him up and flinging him into the air, then catching him and hugging him tightly. She'd seemed so big and strong, like the male Hissa. He wishes he had more memories of her. In comparison, his new owner seems fragile and miniature.

He pushes thoughts of his mother away. Her passing was only the beginning of the Great Death that eventually took the lives of all Hissa females and half the males. That's the very reason for his team's deployment. With a case full of samples and biological data, they were on their way to Bicoma to beg for help.

Bicoma is the home system of an extremely advanced and mysterious species. No one knows how their technology works, or really anything else about them except that they never leave their home solar system. Numerous other races assumed their lack of aggressive expansion meant they would be easy prey. They found out differently when they entered Bicoma space and found their weapons didn't work and ships disappeared.

After extensive negotiations between the Hissa and the Bicoma, his team was granted safe passage into Bicoma space and an audience with the enigmatic species. They'd all been hopeful these secretive creatures might be able to help the Hissa find a solution to their problem.

Somehow, he and his team have failed. Somehow, the ship was captured, and he ended up being sold.

He inspects his new "owner." She is a human female with a long black mane that she's secured high on her head. It flows down from the binding to float around her shoulders and down her back. He doesn't detect any artificial enhancers on her pale face that many other species favor to color their skin or pigment their features. Her eyes are big and expressive, almost too big for the rest of her delicate face. He wants to just gaze at those eyes. They're a deep, rich gold with an auburn ring around the outside edge.

When he leans over a little to get a better look, she doesn't back away. Her expression tells him she's intimidated by him but not afraid. He's not sure why, but he's glad. For some inexplicable reason, he doesn't want her to fear him.

She wears a one-piece biosuit, common with those who work on the smaller spaceships. If she's suddenly exposed to a vacuum, the suit will deploy a small energy helmet to cover her head, protecting her from the harsh void of space. The suit fits her tightly, leaving very little about her shape to the imagination.

He takes a moment to admire her lean, muscular build. She looks and moves like a fighter. Before the Great Death there were female Hissa warriors, and he thinks she might have fit in well within their ranks.

Does she have a male in her life?

He dismisses that idea. If she did, then she wouldn't be wandering alone on this station. Maybe that's why she's buying him, to provide protection for her.

Another thought makes him grow warm. Maybe she wants a sex slave. Perhaps she's lonely and needs companionship. Tiran could do that for her. He's strong, able, and it wouldn't be a hardship to pleasure her. He knows how to give pleasure. He and many other Hissa males make use of the visiting floating brothels that travel from planet to planet. He's bought time with many different species on those ships and learned how to please a human woman.

Maybe he could seduce her into letting the Hissa government buy him back.

Perhaps his captivity won't be so bad.

He grins down at her, uncaring that he's showing her all his teeth.

CHAPTER

3

Mara's eyes go wide when the man's face melts from a snarling mass of teeth to a big smile that transforms his face from predator to puppy.

"I won't hurt you," she tells him quickly in Space Standard, thinking that's the first thing he needs to know. "What's your name?"

"Tree," the big man grunts, his grin disappearing and his face taking on a more guarded expression.

"Tree, as in the plant?" Mara asks, trying to understand his thickly accented Space Standard. Eyes up, she reminds herself when all she wants to do is let her gaze stray down. He's still naked and impressive. Her salacious inner voice is pushing for her to look down.

Just a quick glance.

Shut up, lust; go back into hiding. We're not looking down.

But we own him. Just a little look. It won't hurt him, and then we'll know what we'll be missing when you set him free.

That thought depresses her and makes it easier to keep her eyes on his face.

He's talking again. "No, my name is Tiran," he struggles a bit. Between his accent and search for words, she can tell he doesn't use Space Standard much. "Tiran, it means tree in Hissa. I'm first male of the family Solerion."

Well, at least the name is fitting. The guy's large. "So, you're a Hissa?"

"Yes."

"Ask a stupid question," Mara mutters to herself. "Do you know how you got here?"

"No."

"Are you in any pain?"

"No."

"Do you know what I am? My species?"

"Human." He doesn't spit out the name of her species with disgust, so that's a bonus.

"Not a big talker, are you?" she asks with a rueful grin. Is it her or is he always this taciturn? She can't blame him, being sold has that effect. "I'm Mara. I'm going to take you to my ship. Once we undock, we can talk and figure out what to do with you."

The big man tilts his head and regards her with interest. "Your ship is here?"

"Yes, Witch is secured at dock A, slip 32."

"Is your crew there?" He's asking questions instead of roaring or growling. That has to be a good sign.

"I'm an independent cargo transporter," she explains as she studies him for a moment.

"Are there many crew members?"

"Just me," Mara smiles. "Well, me and the ship. And I guess you too. Look, just follow me and we'll get you some clothes and get you on board. The ship is small, but we should be able to make do." She pauses a moment, thinking about his snarling face from moments ago. He switched from rage to complacent rather fast. He could switch back to rage without any warning. She needs to set down parameters.

"Come with me, and don't make a fuss. I won't hurt you, but if you do try to fight me, I'll be forced to subdue you."

He stiffens, his scales flash brown as he growls at her, baring teeth again. "You would shock me?"

Mara shakes her head violently. "I wouldn't use one of those things," she assures him. "I'd just knock you out with a fist or foot." To her surprise, the big guy smiles again. He doesn't believe she can do it. Well, let him think that. Being underestimated is an excellent advantage.

His scales turn a dark blue as he pointedly looks down at himself. "I would like coverings now."

Following his gaze, she finds her eyes trapped by his massive cock. She might not have much in the way of sexual experience, but when you serve on small ships with predominantly male crews, you see your fair share of naked men. And this man is sporting a work of art dangling between his legs.

What would it look like when it's fully aroused?

Tiran clears his throat, and Mara looks up to find him giving her a knowing look, and his scales flash to purple for a moment, then back to blue.

"Sorry, right, yes," she stammers, feeling her face growing hot. She turns and points to a small shop only a little way from them. "There." Tiran nods and falls in step beside her.

The shop sells mostly biosuits, but they're the sizes that fit tiny Fozin bodies or tall, lean Fieldens. The owner has to dig deep in the back to find a suit large enough to accommodate Tiran's height and bulk. Even wearing the largest size offered in the small shop, it's just shy of too small. The cheap biosuit is stretched so tautly across his big body that she can see the outlines of every one of his lovely muscles and... other things. She can't deny it's a pleasant sight. Still, she wishes there were credits to spare to get him a suit custom made out of better materials, but she's stretching her finances as it is.

Tiran examines the suit, turning around in front of the mirror to make sure the fit's good enough to protect him if the ship suffered a catastrophic failure. He also tests the suit's response by activating it and grunts with satisfaction when it deploys an ion energy helmet correctly.

That's one mystery solved, Mara thinks. He's a seasoned space traveler, not some poor guy kidnapped or sold from a Podunk farm on his home planet.

Now that he's no longer naked, Mara lets herself examine him without guilt. He might be all things massive and muscled, but he also moves with surprising grace. Right now, he's twisting and turning, testing the strength of the suit to make sure it won't split a seam if he does anything more active than standing in front of a mirror. When he bends over, the room seems to get a little warmer.

Licking her lips, her eyes lock on his backside. She wants to grab that ass with both hands and squeeze. The tight suit displays it well and her hands move involuntarily with the thought of massaging all those lovely muscles.

When she drags her gaze back up, Tiran's watching her reflection in the mirror. Their eyes meet, and she can't move. Hell, her lungs even freeze up a little.

His scales flush purple as he slowly smiles at her.

He caught her ogling his ass. She feels her face grow hot. Is she blushing? Again!

What's going on in her world? She never blushes. She never ogles. She doesn't get distracted. She's a hardened spacer. She's fought off raiders. She's killed and come close to being killed on numerous occasions.

And yet this male is making her gawk and blush like

an inept, inexperienced girl.

She turns away from him and focuses on the shop owner. "We'll take it."

She ends up paying far too much for a suit the merchant could never sell, but she doesn't feel she has a choice. He needs clothes and biosuits are an important safety feature in space. She frowns when she checks her remaining balance on her data bracelet. She needs to finish this next run and get paid or there's a high probability of running out of credits for fuel before she finds another contract.

Tiran doesn't comment as they leave the shop. He just silently walks beside her. People stare at the big Hissa as they go by, and Mara finds herself scowling at both men and women as they openly admire his form. Tiran doesn't seem to notice, but Mara's thankful once they're onboard the Witch and he's safely out of sight of prying, lascivious eyes.

She shuts the hatch and turns to tell him she can take off the obedience collar now only to find his bulk rushing at her, arms open, his intent clear.

CHAPTER

4

The moment he finds out the woman has a spaceship and no crew, he decides he'll subdue her and fly her ship back to Hissa instead of the longer process of seduction. He ignores the fact that she cared enough to buy him a biosuit. He isn't familiar with slavery but assumes buying a slave a biosuit is a logical step to safeguard valuable property. Even though he appreciates both being dressed and wearing something essential for most space travel, he hardens himself to what he's going to need to do to this female to gain his freedom.

He promises himself that he'll act honorably toward the female, who's done nothing hurtful or shameful to him yet. He'll restrain her only when he needs to sleep. It'll be a long trip to Hissa, so perhaps he could even persuade her to share his bed when she realizes she's safe with him.

If he's lucky there will only be one bed on her ship and they'll be forced to share. That'll be a delightful problem.

As they draw closer to her docking slip, he decides the best thing to do will be to rush her once they're inside and use his larger size to trap her against the hull of the ship. Once she accepts his dominance, everything will go smoothly.

Perhaps he'll strip her naked too, after all that's what has been done to him. She might even expect it as a captive. He feels himself harden at the thought of her naked. It'll be much easier to entice her to join him for sex if she's naked, and he could better gauge her reaction to him. He knows she likes how he looks. He's caught her staring at him several times now. She turns an odd color when she realizes he's noticed her. He'll have to question her about the color change on their way to Hissa.

He can't wait to hold her naked, lithe body in his arms. He wants to smell her and taste her all over. He's sure she'll taste as wonderful as she looks. A small sting of guilt hits him. He's already planning on having sex with her. That smacks of dishonorable behavior.

No, he won't act dishonorably. He'd never force her. Seduction only. Either she's willing or nothing will happen. It's that simple.

It helps that she's human and not some species he's never encountered before. He's bought time with enough human women at the brothels to know their smell. Hissa males are good at learning scent and how to judge emotions by the smell they produce. He'll find out quickly what pleases the lovely Mara. She won't be able to hide her reactions to him.

All the brothels that visit Hissa employ free individuals. Hissa doesn't allow slavery in their system. Sex workers might start out exaggerating their enjoyment of the act but learn quickly that many species can smell a lack of arousal. Those that enjoy their work get more business and tend to become brutally honest with their clients if asked any questions.

When he paid for time with the human women, he asked a lot of questions. They answered without reserve so he's confident in his knowledge set. After Mara is calm and accepts that he won't hurt her, he can take his time seducing her. It'll be a pleasant way to pass the time, even if she never says yes.

He moves to position himself for attack the moment he enters her ship and waits for her to secure the hatch. He opens his arms wide and checks his speed, he wants to shock her but not hurt her. To his surprise, he runs into the wall.

A blow to his side makes him grunt and turn. There she stands; fists up, legs apart, knees bent, a furious expression on her face.

"You're going to attack me? On my ship? Oh no, you don't, you pile of Pienter shit!" she hisses out.

Tiran's stunned into a moment of stillness. How did she escape him? He knows he's fast. He's always been fast. Faster than many of the other Hissa warriors. He has to be. He's short for a Hissa male and to be competitive he had to make himself much faster than his larger, stronger competitors.

Perhaps he's weak from being woken so abruptly from a sleep pod. And no one gave him food or water since he woke. He's not in peak condition. No matter, he'll catch her.

He rushes her again, and this time he's barely able to follow her movement as she ducks around him and delivers another blow to his rib cage. He's able to grab her wrist only to have her jab him in the face with her free hand.

Pain explodes behind his eyes, and he tastes blood in his mouth as she breaks out of his grip. This female is far more skilled in hand-to-hand combat than he anticipated. No wonder she was so confident earlier.

This is a bad situation. Her skill means he might need to hit her. The pain in his face is a harsh wake-up call to her fighting ability and his weakened state.

He strikes out with an open hand, hoping to stun her, but she's able to dodge him. Her hair brushes his hand as she moves out of the way of his strike. He grunts with pain as she delivers two more sharp jabs to his ribs and a kick to his knee. He staggers but doesn't fall. Pain radiates from his ribs and face.

She's damaging him! How can this small female throw such a strong punch?

She dances away from him, and he sees her look to her right. He follows her face and notices a small blue drug box mounted to the wall. The box, containing pre-loaded drug guns full of powerful sedatives, is required by Space Standard law in most systems. Passengers or fellow crew can be violent for any number of reasons, and quick sedation assures everyone's safety.

Understanding her intention, he moves between her and the drug box. The space inside the cabin is small, giving him the advantage.

"Submit!" he growled at her.

"The way I see it," she tells him grimly, her gaze steady and her posture defiant, "you're the one who should be submitting. Just wait till I've got you down. I'm going to make you regret this."

She should be showing more fear. She should be terrified of his size and strength considering he towers over her. Instead, she stands centered and ready, a true warrior. Shame fills Tiran, both for his lack of skills at the moment and the fact that he's fighting her at all.

No, what he's doing is necessary. He dismisses the feeling of guilt as he snaps an arm out. She ducks away, he follows but he continues with a follow-up maneuver that manages to trap her in the narrow section near the hatch. He feels triumph for only a moment. Then she's using him as a ladder, climbing up his chest with a speed he's ill-prepared for. Belatedly, he reaches up to grab her only to feel her jump from his shoulders.

He turns in time to see her execute a flip and land crouched behind him. He expects her to spring up and move away. Instead, she lashes out with one of her feet and catches him in his uninjured leg.

Agony makes him roar as he falls, his natural grace deserting him. Hitting the ground hard knocks the wind out of him. Fighting off the stunning effects of the fall, he tries to regain his feet. The last thing he feels is the sting of the drug gun against his neck, and then the world fades to black.

CHAPTER 5

Breathing raggedly, Mara slumps down on the floor next to Tiran and glares at the unconscious Hissa.

"I was doing you a favor!" she hisses at his unconscious form as she tries to catch her breath. She never expected a guy his size to be so fast. Her speed is her strongest asset. Few can match her. Tiran came uncomfortably close.

Leaning over, she strokes Witch's hull. "It's okay," she assures the ship. "I won't let him steal you from me." She feels a grumble of contentment come from the ship, making her smile.

Witch wasn't sure what was going on during the fight, so she remained still and silent while Mara and Tiran battled it out. If the big Hissa had managed to knock Mara out, the ship could've reacted very badly, and it'd be unlikely either Tiran or she would have survived. She needs to start training Witch to restrain intruders. However, in her defense, this is the first time she's ever been attacked on her ship. It's not a scenario she thought would happen.

Witch could learn to work with Mara, herding intruders into the cargo bay and caging them there. They could even get a self-propelling practice dummy to work this. Not that Mara ever plans on letting a stranger into Witch ever again. This big Hissa taught her a valuable lesson; she and Witch should be prepared for anything the universe might throw at them.

And training will keep Witch from potentially panicking and turning herself inside out. Living ships instinctively do that in moments of extreme stress. Nothing good can come from a terrified or hysterical living ship.

"Don't worry, sweet Witch," she coos to the ship. "It's you and me forever." Living ships like Witch are rare because they're easy to kill with harsh handling. Living ships, cultivated from giant seeds, and given frames to grow into, have to be coaxed and cared for or they just wither and die. Mara bought Witch when the ship was on the brink of death. It took almost a Space Standard year to nurse the ship back to health, but the bond between them flowered.

Because of the trust between them, Witch has willingly flown Mara into situations most living ships would refuse to enter and many inorganic ships would never be able to handle. The two of them don't just survive; they thrive.

Mara looks back at Tiran and sighs. She really can't blame the guy for trying to escape. In his shoes, she would do the same thing. Hell, she *has* done the same thing, killing several people in the process.

That brings to mind the uncomfortable question of what to do with him now. She wants to just open the hatch and dump him back on the space station. But even if she ends the slave contract, he's vulnerable. Most of these space stations are just a half step from lawlessness, and he could easily be swallowed back into the slave market.

From the way he acted at the auction, it's obvious he doesn't know how to play the slave game. He has no idea how to survive in this kind of world. Leaving him would be a death sentence. Despite his attempt to take her ship, Mara still feels sympathy for the Hissa.

If she isn't going to leave him on the station, that means she's taking him with her. It's only a few days to her next port. She'll unload her cargo, get paid, give him a little money, and leave him there to find his own way home.

Having a plan makes her feel better. Now she just has to

figure out how to keep this Hissa out of trouble for the next few days.

She staggers to her feet and takes a few deep breaths to stop the shaking. Adrenaline is still ricocheting through her system, and it makes her slightly unsteady now that the fight's over. She knows from experience she'll need to lie down soon. Her odd genetics make her vulnerable after the stress of a battle is over.

All humans might suffer from fatigue after an adrenaline rush, but for Mara and her sister Lara, the crash after an adrenaline high is extreme. Very soon she'll need to rest and while she sleeps, nothing will wake her up. Honestly, calling it sleep doesn't do it justice. To her it feels like she slips into a short-term coma.

Tiran needs to be secured quickly before she succumbs to her genetics.

"Witch, undock and head to next coordinates," she orders. She hears the clunk of the docking clamps being released and then a gentle acceleration as Witch moves them away from the dock with minimal power. Once she's at a safe distance, Witch will fire up the main thrusters and perform a full burn for several minutes to launch them toward their next port.

She can ignore the ship now. Witch will perform perfectly without any more instructions or guidance from Mara. That frees her up to figure out how to secure her dangerous guest. Walking into the cargo bay, she starts searching for anything she can use to bind the Hissa snoring away on the floor of her cabin. She finds several straps not currently in use to hold down cargo and cuts them into usable lengths.

Carrying her improvised restraints back into the cabin, she contemplates Tiran's inert form. She looks over at her bunk, back at Tiran, then back to the bunk. She only has one bed on the ship and no couch or chairs other than the captain's chair. She never travels with companions so there's been no need for more. If she ties Tiran to the bed, then she'll have to spend a few uncomfortable sleep days on the floor or in the captain's chair.

She briefly looks over to the cargo hold but dismisses it. She can't bring herself to tie him in the cargo hold. Witch isn't set up to regulate the temperature in there, so it's always very cold. Not to mention that if something breaks loose during maneuvering, it might kill him. Besides, she doesn't like the idea of him sleeping on the harsh metal grates in there.

Taking hold of an arm, she tries to drag Tiran to the bunk but finds his dead weight just won't budge. "Damn, you're massive," she mutters. "Witch, is there any way you can get this guy on the bunk without hurting him?"

The ship gives a little sound that tells Mara it's thinking. After a few tentative shifts the floor starts to gently rise under Tiran. Once the floor has him about four feet high, it stops rising. For a moment Mara thinks Witch's solution to her request is to make a 'bed' under where he is, instead of trying to get him on her bunk. Witch can be a little too smart for her own good and sometimes finds 'creative' solutions to Mara's demands.

But she shouldn't have doubted Witch in this instance. The floor starts to shift and change again. A platform raises up, spanning the distance between Tiran and the bunk. Mara isn't sure what her ship is attempting until one side of the platform starts to gradually curve. Tiran's body slides down the curve toward the bunk. Witch glides his big body into the bunk with barely a jostle. Once he's safely stowed on the bunk, the platform and slide recede into the floor.

"Well done!" Mara cheers. "You're such a smart ship!" The ship gives a contented grumble around her, and Mara smiles with delight. "Let me get this guy secured, and I'll give you the present I picked up on the station." The ship quakes a little, and Mara knows it's from excitement. Witch loves her presents.

Picking up the straps, Mara makes quick work of securing both Tiran's arms and legs. Once done, she sits on the edge of the bunk and takes a good look. Despite the earlier violence, her hands itch to touch him. She doesn't. But it's a near thing. She has no intentions of violating the body of a helpless man, but she has to admit this is the first time she's felt so drawn to anyone. He even smells good.

She leans over and takes a deep breath through her nose. The man just came from a slave auction. How can he smell this enticing?

Of course, however good he might look and smell, she's going to need to lay down the law once he wakes up. No one attacks her on her ship. This idiot got himself a one-way trip to the next station tied to a bunk.

Witch rumbles impatiently, and Mara chuckles. "I'm getting it!" she calls out.

Standing up she tries to walk but ends up stumbling for a step. She's starting to feel the effects of the fight. She fishes around in her pocket until she finds the small square of metal she bought while waiting for the slave auction. Making her way to the front, she opens a compartment in the control console and drops the cube of rare metal in. The fleshy inside of the compartment closes over the cube, and it disappears. Witch gives a tinkling sound of delight.

"I know," Mara murmurs to the ship with a broad smile. "I didn't think I'd find terium around here either. Enjoy it, sweetheart. We probably won't find it again for a while."

Snoring draws her attention back to Tiran. "And you enjoy your nap, handsome," she says to her unconscious passenger as she settles down in the captain's chair. Suddenly she's so exhausted she can't keep her eyes open any longer. "I promise Witch and I will make the ride as smooth as possible. You just stay out of trouble."

CHAPTER

6

A roar loud enough to vibrate her chair wakes Mara. Jumping to her feet, fists in the air and ready to fight, she looks wildly around for the threat. When she realizes it's Tiran making all the noise, her fear turns to annoyance. Looks like the big guy is awake and objecting to his current state. He's fighting violently against his bonds. It's a good thing the bunk is part of the ship's hull, or he would've already ripped it apart.

He roars again and despite all her training and experience, she flinches at the sound. This guy's vocal cords are intense. Then Witch gives an unhappy wobble, and Mara rushes to Tiran's side.

"Stop it!" she orders. "You're upsetting the ship."

"Untie me!" he thunders, and the ship shakes again. He's covered in sweat and straining his massive, muscled body against his bonds with enough force to make the straps narrow.

"Stop scaring the ship!" Mara shouts right into his face and that seems to startle him.

He stops struggling and glares at her, "Scare ship? What speaking about?" His rage is making his accent thicker than it was on the space station, and he's mangling sentence structure, but at least she can still understand him. "Can't scare ship. You scared. Good, let me go!"

"No, you idiot, you can scare a ship. Witch is a living ship. Your shouting and struggling is upsetting her." Mara glares right back at him. "If you upset her enough, she'll turn herself inside out. Then we get to hang out in space and hope the air in our biosuits lasts long enough for her to calm down, right herself, and collect us."

Tiran blanches, his scale pattern going from black to a deep blue. "Why you bring me on such ship?" He lowers his voice to just above a whisper, making Mara fight back a smile.

"You don't need to whisper. Just don't roar anymore. Witch is the best ship you will ever have the privilege to ride in," she tells him proudly. She reaches out to stroke the hull near the bunk. "You're a good ship. I promise more treats at the next port." The ship sounds a contented murmur and the quaking stops.

Mara looks back at Tiran to see his eyes are wide with shock. "I've heard of such, but I've never been on one." His accent is getting a little less thick, and he's starting to structure his sentences better. He must be calming down.

"Tiran meet Witch." Mara pulls her hand away from the hull and rests it on Tiran's chest. "Witch meet Tiran. He won't make any more loud, scary noises, and he absolutely won't attack me again."

That statement brings Tiran's scowl back. "No more loudness. You can release me."

She doesn't move, just asks him one simple question. "Why?" Tiran looks confused and again Mara bites her lip to keep from smiling.

"Because—" he starts, then seems to flail about for an answer. "I don't like it."

"Right," Mara gives him a sardonic look. "I'm not too fond of being attacked on my ship either. Now you're stuck with the consequences."

Both of them are quiet for a moment, and then suddenly Tiran's face softens, and his scale pattern turns a light purple. "I could pleasure you."

He rolls his eyes down to draw her attention to where her hand still rests on his chest. She snatches her hand away and gapes at him. "What the hell do you mean by that?" Of all the tactics she thought he might use; seduction isn't one of them.

"You have no male, and we are here together. Untie me, and I can entertain you. I'm very good. I've practiced on humans before."

"Slaves," Mara states woodenly. Most brothels exclusively use slaves to service clients. She always considered herself very lucky never to have ended up in one.

"Never," Tiran spat out. "I'd never do that. My friends and I would go to the independent floating brothels when they visited our planet. The Allure was my favorite. The female I spent the night with the last time was human. She was very," he pauses as if looking for the right word in Space Standard, "demanding."

"Oh," Mara feels both relief and annoyance. She's delivered to the Allure and knows the place is run fairly. Everyone working there is doing it by choice, not force.

Then the image of Tiran with one of the Allure women pops in her head. Did the woman enjoy it or just pretend to? She wonders what sex with something as big and masculine as this Hissa would be like. Probably one wild ride.

Tiran's nose flares, and he grins, the purple of his scale pattern darkening. "Would you be demanding too?" he asks and moves his body a little, so his hip rubs against her leg. She jumps off the bed as if his touch burns.

"No, no," she says quickly and tucks her hands in her pockets before she gives in to the temptation to touch him.

"Bad, bad, bad."

Tiran frowns and shakes his head. "I assure you I'm good. I've been told this repeatedly."

"No, I mean it would be a bad idea for us. We aren't… we shouldn't…." Mara stops talking as she feels her face getting hot. She takes a deep breath and tries again.

"You're tied down, and it wouldn't be appropriate for me to…" She stops again and wants to hit herself. Space Standard is one of a dozen languages that were programmed in her brain before she was even Decanted. Why is she struggling with it now? What the hell is wrong with her? "Look, no touching. We are not doing that."

"You could untie me," Tiran suggests.

Feeling on firmer ground here, she shakes her head. "There is no way that's going to happen, big guy. You're faster than I expected, and I'm not taking any chances. Once we get to Gleem, I'll head into the station, and once I'm gone, Witch can untie you so you can leave. I'm not going to take the risk of tangling with you again."

Tiran looks like he is about to argue but instead runs his gaze up and down her. His gaze is openly admiring but not in a sexual way. It feels like he's reassessing her as an opponent. His scale pattern goes back to blue as he examines her. She's getting the feeling dark blue is the default color, and all the other color changes are caused by emotional reaction.

"You're much more skilled and faster than I expected," he admits. "A strong warrior." There's admiration in his voice. "You're small and should be weak and easy to defeat. But I couldn't seem to catch you. Where did you learn such things?"

Mara debates telling him the truth. It might make him feel safer to know her history, but she hates the pitying looks people give her when they find out about her and her sister.

Tiran waits patiently for her to talk. He doesn't try and cajole her or threaten, just stares at her with quiet intensity.

It suddenly occurs to her that this Hissa's been through a lot. He's lost everything, was sold at an auction, and really couldn't have known she wasn't going to do something horrible to him the moment she got him on the ship. She should have anticipated his attack and taken measures sooner to either make sure he couldn't attack or assured him he was safe.

Now he could use that reassurance. She can't think of anything more that would cement the fact she wouldn't hurt someone vulnerable than sharing her own story.

"I'm Decanted," she starts.

"Decanted?" Tiran repeats. His brow ridge furrows in confusion.

"Human scientists figured out how to grow fetuses in vats. At first it was done to provide rich couples with children but with none of the fuss or mess of pregnancy or childbirth. It didn't take very long for businessmen to figure out there was more profit to be made by growing designer slaves."

She turns so her right side is visible. Pulling her ear forward, she points to a scar that runs from behind her ear all the way down the back of her neck.

"This is a Decanting scar. All of us have them. It's from the machines they use to monitor and develop our brains while we are being grown. It allows them to program us with language and skills. My sister and I were programmed with a lot of languages but not much else because our owners didn't request or pay for extra training."

"You were created to be a slave." Tiran moves against the straps, agitated. "What was your purpose?"

"They called our kind Decade Children," Mara explains. "Decade Children are a big fad on Mavus and other planets in that sector. They combined a bunch of different

DNAs to make us appear childlike longer and implanted several devices that pumped a steady stream of puberty suppressing hormones into our systems. Most human females go through puberty somewhere between 13 to 16 years old. We were about twenty-five when my sister and I started puberty."

A look of utter disgust appears on Tiran's face. "There were men who wanted to bed children?"

Mara forces herself not to react to Tiran's statement. It's what everyone always assumes. "We weren't created for sex. We were decorations. If you're rich and live on a planet like Mavus you're supposed to own a bunch of exotic slaves that have little or no purpose. It's a display of wealth. My sister and I were very expensive to buy, and we would be trotted out for social gatherings or parties." Mara shrugs. "It wasn't a bad life for a slave. We were mostly bored."

She decides not to mention the intense pain they suffered occasionally from the implants and hormones or the discipline she and her sister suffered at the hands of one of the family's sadistic butlers. Some things are better left unsaid, and many slaves live much worse lives.

"You are here. An adult female with a ship. How?"

Mara takes a deep breath and debates whether to continue telling her story or not. Now that he knows she'd been a slave it might be enough to make him understand he's safe with her even while being secured to the bunk. But she finds she wants to tell her story to this Hissa. For the first time she wants to share.

And it has been a long time since she had someone besides Witch to talk to.

"Lara, my twin sister, and I hit puberty at the same time. The family was lax in updating our implants. We went from having the appearance of six-year-olds to what you see now in less than a year." Mara pauses, looking for the right words. "It was unpleasant." That's a gross understatement. If not for the kindness of the other slaves both sisters would have died. Sometimes the pain was so bad Mara wished someone would just kill her.

Tiran looks angry for a moment, and Mara wonders why, but his next words explain it. "They could have eased you into your growth over many years. That didn't need to happen."

Touched, Mara gives him a bitter smile. "They could've, but that would've deprived them of their expensive property that much sooner. We were very lucky. The owners were on an extended trip to a nearby planet, so they didn't know it happened until they got back. By then we could move and care for ourselves again. If it had happened while they'd been in residence we would probably have been disposed of."

Tiran hisses and strains against his straps. He says something violently in Hissa. Mara rears back, worrying he'll start fighting the straps again. Tiran sees her movement and relaxes his arms back onto the bunk. "I'm angry for you. I'm angry for slaves. No life should be treated so casually."

With a nod of agreement, she sits back down on the edge of the bed. "I'm in total agreement with you on that score, handsome."

"You call me handsome," he smirks. "You find my appearance pleasing?"

"And here's where I ignore that line of questioning," she retorts.

His smirk doesn't diminish. "We can discuss it later if you like." She watches as his scales change to purple around the outside. By now she's sure black means rage and purple probably means sexual interest.

"Sure. Much, much later," she agrees and feels a little relief when the purple edges of his scale pattern turn back to blue. *Like after I drop you off on Gleem*, she adds silently.

"I wish to know more. How did you get your freedom?" His voice is interested, and his body is still relaxed. She's willing to answer these questions if it'll keep him calm and keeps them off the topic of how delectable she finds him.

"We didn't have any more value to them, so they sold us to one of those brothels. One of the nasty places that goes through a lot of slaves because the clients like to be rough." Mara's explanation is interrupted when Tiran growls again.

"Don't get all noisy," she admonishes him with a grin. "This is the best part of the story. It turns out whatever genetic combo we are made from to give us childlike features and stunt our growth for so long made us fast and strong once we had adult bodies. The guys we were sold to decided to play with us the minute the ship was on course for the brothel. I fought back and managed to fling a guy across the cabin. It surprised all of us. It was a short melee after that. I ended up killing those guys pretty quickly. It was just the four of us on board: the two guys that bought us and me and my sister. With the guys dead, we were suddenly free."

"You killed them. That's good," Tiran grunts.

Mara smiles at the happy memory. "The three weeks we had on that ship were the best time of my life."

Tiran frowns, thinking about her story. "You were on your way to being sold. You were attacked and forced to kill to defend yourself. I find little to be happy about in that."

"I know, but you have to look at it from our point of view. After we flushed the bodies out of the airlock, the ship was ours. All ours. We ate, talked, slept, and never had to worry about an owner getting mad. For the first time in our lives, we owned ourselves."

"But did you know how to pilot?" Tiran's question is knowing.

Smile fading, she gives a little shrug. "Of course not. We wouldn't even have known how to read or write if it hadn't been programmed into us while we were being grown in the vat. But we were young and thought we could make it. We didn't have much experience in space and if the ship hadn't already been set up on autopilot, we would've probably crashed within hours of taking over. We couldn't even figure out how to reprogram the autopilot."

Tiran eyes her with pity. "That means you were still flying to the brothel."

She gives him a rueful look. "Yup. Nothing we could do about it, so we came up with a plan."

"Plan?"

"Yeah, a scheme to make it out with our freedom intact and maybe even keep the ship. Looking back, I understand how naive we were, but at the time it seemed like a good idea. We couldn't change the ship's course, so we were going to dock with the brothel and pretend we were the slavers looking to buy instead of sell."

Tiran's thick brow ridge rises, and it looks very similar to when a human raises an eyebrow. She's pretty sure that look translates to incredulous. "That wouldn't have worked."

Mara rolls her eyes. "Well, I know that now. But remember, at that point we knew very little of how the galaxy worked outside of our little corner. Anyway, do you want to know the rest or not?"

Schooling his features to present her with a neutral expression, he nods. "Please continue. I won't interrupt again."

"There isn't much more to tell. We got attacked by raiders, and my sister and I jumped into life pods. The next thing I know, I'm being picked up by some rescue ship. They were Fieldens so they were all about refugees. I was afraid to say anything and end up back a slave so I pretended I couldn't speak. They just assumed I was damaged and might never be fully functional again. I didn't have an ID chip in me anymore and the state of my clothes made them think I was probably some kind of agricultural worker being transferred from one planet to another. Just cheap labor that survived the destruction of a labor transport ship. The same raiders that attacked us had attacked three other ships in the same area."

"I was taken down to the planet, issued an ID, and told to report to the Department of Restructuring for housing and an assignment. It's standard procedure for any Fielden refugee or citizen with severe damage and no family. I took the bag of stuff they issued to me and headed straight to the nearest spaceport. Gave myself the last name Lost, because that's how I felt without my sister Lara, and talked myself into a job. I've been working in space and looking for my sister ever since. I saved up a little money and got a great deal on Witch because she was in such bad shape when I bought her."

"You've created resources where there were none to use," Tiran declares approvingly. "You're a clever, determined female."

"It's amazing what you can do when you have nothing to lose," Mara points out with a grin.

"But you're more than just resourceful. You also fight very well."

Mara flushes with pleasure at the compliment. "Thanks. I worked very hard on it the entire time I was a slave."

Tiran looks confused. "Your owner wanted you to be able to fight?"

Mara chuckles at the misunderstanding. "No way. We were supposed to be walking dolls. Some of the outfits they put us in had so many flourishes we couldn't move very well.

But there was a lot of downtime, and it got boring for the slaves and staff. My sister liked reading and hung out with the family's tutor, but I liked to fight. The family had a massive gym they rarely used. They also hired a full-time fighting instructor to train their lazy kid. The guy was bored too, so one day when he found me in the gym trying to copy moves that I saw in vids, he decided he'd train me. No one said I couldn't, and he was free and a highly prized instructor. He could have quit at any time and gone to work for another wealthy family, so we were ignored." Mara grins at the memory.

"This instructor treated you as a child of the family, not a slave," Tiran guessed.

"He did. It also helped that I was so tiny they figured no matter how much training I got, I'd still be easy to subdue because of my small stature. Even my training was amusing to them. A toy doing something unexpected." She shrugs at the memory. "At the time, I couldn't have cared less what they said because it meant I got to spend a lot of my downtime training. My sister would join occasionally, but she liked to read and fiddle with stuff. She's smart too, smarter than me. She became good at taking things apart and figuring out how they worked. She even started fixing things the family discarded. The cook started coming to her when things malfunctioned in the kitchen. Most of the staff were kind to us so she liked doing them favors. But I couldn't sit still long enough to learn like she did. And Captain Dolan was all about movement."

Mara hadn't thought about Captain Dolan, the fighting instructor, in a long time. He'd been like a father to her. He didn't just teach fighting. He explained a lot of basics about life outside of the family compound. He was the one who'd explained what it was like to be free. Looking back, Mara now understood he treated her like the growing child she was instead of a pretty decoration. He was visiting his own family when they were sold, or she's sure he would've bought her and Lara himself.

Once she and Witch started hauling cargo, she tried to find Captain Dolan. But no one knew where he retired to. The thought of never getting to thank him and tell him how important he was to her childhood rankled, but she pushed it aside. When there's nothing to be done about the past, there's no point in pushing it into the present.

"I've made you sad," Tiran says, pulling her out of her memories.

"No, I'm fine," she says quickly. "I know you can't be super comfortable but how about a snack? I've got meal bars. I'll even let you have the chocolate flavor, that one almost tastes like food."

She expects him to protest, to demand to be let loose again, but he doesn't.

He stares are her intensely for so long she gets uncomfortable. She can't read the expression on his face, but it almost seems like a combination of interest and sympathy. "I could get you a drink if you're thirsty. I've got sealed packets with built-in straws so you can drink without too much mess."

Still, he doesn't speak, and Mara watches his facial expression change again, interest still there, but also a kind of determination. No change in his scale pattern so that's no help. She wishes she knew what he was thinking. "Hello? You hungry? Thirsty? Tired? I can lower the lights so you can sleep."

"You may release me," he finally states with calm demand. It's as if he's asking her to pass something over to him at a meal. "I believe your story and won't attack you. I'll act as your crew on this voyage. I'm skilled at programming and can operate many different types of machines."

"We've been over that," Mara tells him gently. She hopes he doesn't start roaring and struggling again. "I can't risk it. I promise you'll be free soon. Just a few days and I'll drop you off on Gleem."

To her relief Tiran doesn't protest her decision. He takes a deep breath of air and regards her with a tender expression. His hour-glass shaped pupils don't waver from her gaze and his sharp canines stay hidden behind closed lips. The scale pattern on his head remains a dark blue, telling her he's probably as calm as he's acting.

That's good. If he stays calm, the journey will be much easier.

"I accept my captivity, and I'm sorry I attacked you." He closes his eyes. His expression is desolate. "This is a fitting punishment for my actions. If you feel the need, you may hurt me now also. I promise to remain quiet. I forfeit myself to you."

CHAPTER

7

Opening his eyes, Tiran watches Mara's face flush with outrage and bites back a smile.

"I'm not punishing you!" She tells him hotly. "And I'm certainly not going to torture you or anything like that."

"I deserve this," he insists and makes sure his voice sounds despondent. "I'll understand if you don't wish to share your resources with me for our voyage to Gleem. I don't deserve care. I'm strong. I can survive the trip with no sustenance."

Scowling, Mara crosses her arms over her chest. "Stop it!" she demands. "Look, I did offer to feed you. I just can't risk untying you right now. But that's not because I want to hurt you. I'm not trying to punish you."

Tiran decides he needs a little more dramatic flourish. "Among the Hissa, I've dishonored myself," he scrambles to think of something and then almost breaks character and grins when an idea occurs to him. "I wear a collar. I've been bought and sold. I was defeated by a female opponent. I'm no longer worthy to live among my people. Do with me as you wish. I'll not object."

He watches Mara's agitated movement at his words and knows he's hitting the right chord with her.

"Slavery is done to us," she protests. "It's not like anyone wakes up and just decides being a slave is a great idea. I'm sure your people will understand. And if they don't, then fuck them! Besides, how can they even know? I won't tell anyone, and your sale record begins and ends on that station. It's not like there's a central slave database or anything."

She pulls something out of her pocket and then moves closer and reaches for his throat. He tenses, worried about what she's doing, but he only hears a clink and then feels her lift the collar away.

"See," she holds up the open collar for him to see. "No collar. Not a slave anymore. You're good to go!"

"It doesn't change my failures. I'll be an outcast." Tiran wonders if he might have gone a little too far when Mara looks apoplectic, but her next words fill him with relief.

"Pienter shit!" she exclaims, and he pretends to draw away from her, casting his eyes down as if unworthy to meet her gaze. Using his peripheral vision, he watches her fight to control her anger.

"Look, if your people are that bad, then you don't need to go back there. There're plenty of jobs to be had, especially if you've got programming skills. I even had to hire outside programmers for Witch's navigation computer a couple of times. You could get yourself a nice independent gig on a repair station. They're always short of skilled labor."

He raises his eyes and gives her his best pleading expression. "I could work for you. I could help you in your travels." Leaning back, Mara eyes him suspiciously, and Tiran curses himself silently for pushing too quickly. He should've been more patient. He backpedals.

"You are disgusted by me. I understand. No one would want me touching their ship. I'm one of the Dishonored." He mentally pats himself on the back for that idea. It sounds heart-wrenching. In truth it was almost impossible to become an outcast on Hissa. They aren't a numerous species and communities are tightly knit. Fights can break out, especially among young males, but it's always handled with arbitration until both families are satisfied. Mara doesn't know much about his species or culture.

"I don't need any crew," Mara tells him. "But I guess you can help me while we travel to Gleem. Let me get these off, and maybe you can look at one of the thruster feeds. It keeps jamming, and I've replaced it at least three times."

Remaining perfectly still, he watches Mara release the bonds. He's going to need to be very careful with the next part. Once the bonds are undone Mara jumps away, as if expecting an attack. Her face is anxious, and her hands are already curled into fists, ready for a confrontation.

Pretending he doesn't see her preparing for battle, he sits up slowly, clutching his side as if in pain. It's true he does hurt where Mara landed several powerful blows, but it's only discomfort, not the agony he's feigning.

He makes sure pain shows on his face when he looks up at her. "Show me to the control console." Making a show of trying to stand, he drops back down on the bunk as if dizzy. His ruse is rewarded when Mara rushes to him and gently urges him to lie flat again, even going so far as to grab his legs and heave them up on the bunk.

"You might have taken some damage during the fight. Where does it hurt?" she asks, distress making her words rapid.

Dropping his head back, he closes his eyes and gives a small groan.

Her hands on his face are gentle, and her smell fills his nose. By the moons, she smells good. It takes an inordinate amount of willpower to keep from turning his head to nuzzle her arm.

"I think you've got a fever." Her voice is filled with concerned agitation.

Leaning a little closer, she runs her hand over his forehead and skull. She doesn't wear any scent-altering substances, thankfully, because the natural smell of her body is intoxicating all by itself. It's interesting: the human sex workers on the Allure didn't smell anywhere near as good as Mara. Maybe it's because she's Decanted, and her DNA isn't fully human. Whatever the reason, he pulls her scent into his lungs and lets it heat his skin with desire.

She gives a little gasp as his flesh warms under her hands. "I can feel your fever getting worse! Damn, I'm going to need to find a medical suite. And your scales have gone purple. Does it do that when you're sick too?"

Remembering from one of his classes as a child that Hissa have a higher standing body temperature than many other species, he uses her lack of knowledge to his advantage. "It's hot in here. Perhaps the temperature control system is malfunctioning. I'll look at that too. Let me just rest for a moment and then I'll see to it."

He pauses, then adds, "I'll be useful to you, I promise. You won't need to send me away. Don't waste your credits on a medical suite for me. I'm not worth it. I'll survive this. Don't send me away. Don't discard me."

With an irritated sound she pets his head with gentle hands. "I won't just abandon you. Gleem is a big station, tons of traffic. I'm sure we can find you a job there if you don't want to go home. Or find you passage home if you're ready to go back to your people by the time we get there. But we can worry about that later. Let's try and figure out what's causing you that pain and fever first."

He doesn't open his eyes at her encouraging words. Pretending he's in pain, he gives another small groan. "My chest hurts."

She runs her hands over his chest, feeling for anything obvious. Her touch, even through the biosuit, sends a hot wave of sensation through his body. He can feel his shaft getting hard. He rolls on his side and pulls up his legs to hide the erection.

Standing up, she moves away from the bunk. He risks opening his eyes to watch her pull a med kit from one of the storage compartments. He schools his features to show pain when she turns around.

"I've got a basic med kit. It should be able to detect any internal bleeding or broken bones," she says. "There's a moon with a large enough population to have a dedicated medical suite, and it's not too far from here. If we find anything bad, we can head there."

Kneeling next to him, she opens the box. The hand scanner is one of the cheaper models, and it sounds several angry beeps when she tries to run it over him. "Damn it," she curses, then puts her hand on his face, cupping his cheek. She gives him a reassuring smile. "I'm going to need to take your biosuit off. Just the top. This scanner can't read through it. I promise not to do anything else to you."

It's all Tiran can do to hide his glee. "If you must," he manages to say with resignation. He feels his arousal getting worse as she starts to undo the various fasteners on the suit. He wonders how badly she'll react if she sees his stiff member. Maybe he can convince her it needs to be very thoroughly checked for injury also.

He watches her tug, pull, and grunt through half-closed eyes as she struggles to get the suit off him. "Can you lever yourself up on your arm? I think I can get your top off if I can just get that fastener at your waist."

"I will comply." He makes his arm shake a little as he holds himself up.

"Got it!" she tells him, and he lets himself fall back down with an exaggerated sigh of relief as if the effort has been too much for him. He feels her soft hands on his head again, stroking from his forehead to the nape of his neck. "It's going to be fine," she promises him in a whisper close to his ear. "You'll be up and moving in no time."

A momentary flash of guilt goes through him at the deception, but it passes once her hands are on the skin of his bare chest. He almost groans from her touch, and it takes every last shred of willpower he has to keep from moving his hips. Not only has it been a long time since he bedded a female, but this one seems different. Her smell is sweeter, and her touch makes him feel things he's never felt with anyone else.

She withdraws her hands, and then the medical scanner is on his skin. He can feel the slight pressure as she moves it along his body. "No broken bones, but it looks like I might have cracked a couple of your ribs," she murmurs to him. He's not surprised she managed to do that much damage. Her blows were accurate and powerful. If he wasn't trained to keep his chin lowered during a battle, she might have been able to land one of those blows on his neck, potentially incapacitating or even killing him.

Remembering her fighting skills doesn't diminish his ardor. If anything, he feels his body flush with even more excitement. She'd probably be just as fierce in bed as she is in battle.

"Looks like some bad bruising, no bleeding. All your organs look good. So, you're probably feeling the effects of the drugs they gave you before the auction."

Tiran doesn't remember being given anything, not even food or water. "Drugs?"

"Most slave auctions use calming drugs to keep everything nice and smooth during the auction. They probably hit you with the drug in a shock stick, but your genetics are just different enough so the drug affected you in ways it normally wouldn't with most slaves. It might be upping your pain receptors." She reaches up and strokes his chest, and he almost purrs with the feel of it. "I'm sorry. It's a bad deal. You're just going to need to sleep it off."

Alarm goes through him as she reaches for the med box again. "Don't make me sleep." His voice comes out far too harsh, and she freezes. He softens his tone and makes his face appear anxious. "I was traveling in a sleep pod with my crew, and the next thing I knew, I was being woken and sold. Don't make me sleep with drugs I can't wake from."

Her cautious expression is replaced with understanding, and she gives him a reassuring smile. "How about a mild pain reliever? I'm not sure it will work on you, but it shouldn't make you sleepy or anything like that."

Tiran considers it and nods. "Yes, that would be good."

Showing him the medication so he can approve it first, she injects him and then pats his arm. "That should help."

Reaching out, he captures her hand. Ignoring the way she tenses at his touch; he pulls her hand to his head. "Please touch me again. I feel unsettled. Your touch is a comfort."

Making a small sound of surprise, she obediently starts petting him. "I promise things will work out," she whispers to him.

"I'm very glad you bought me. I promise to be a good investment." To his disappointment, she abruptly withdraws her hand at his words and stands up. He might have played that last bit a little too subservient.

"You rest, big guy," she tells him as she hastily gathers up the med kit. "We'll figure it all out later."

He wants to protest the loss of her touch but suddenly feels exhausted. The pain relievers are doing their job, making him realize he's been effectively ignoring a lot of pain. He falls asleep to the thought that perhaps, if he's very lucky, he'll wake up to find Mara had joined him in the bunk. That puts a smile on his face.

CHAPTER

8

    Again, Mara finds herself watching Tiran as he sleeps. Who smiles in their sleep? How can he snore and smile at the same time?

    He's been out for hours, and even though she should be doing repairs and general maintenance, she keeps finding herself staring at the slumbering Hissa.

    Annoyed with herself, she decides to at least check on the cargo hold when Witch suddenly gives a violent shake. Shrill alarms sound in the cabin, and Mara rushes to the control console. Lights and warnings are flashing everywhere. She curses herself for not getting a proper console connected to Witch. Because Witch has only minimal interface components with the computer, she doesn't have the ability to tell Mara exactly what's gone wrong. She just sets off every alarm she's hooked to.

    Straightening up from the console, she bumps right into something solid behind her. Fearful that Witch is so damaged that the hull's failing, she ducks down, ready to dash aside to avoid anything falling on her.

"I'm not attacking you!" a voice bellows at her. Mara looks up to find Tiran looming over her. Damn, the guy is big. She stands up and leans close so he can hear her over the wailing alarms.

"There's something wrong with Witch," she screams.

"I guessed that," Tiran shouts back with an exasperated expression.

If their situation wasn't so dire Mara would be laughing at this exchange. "No, I mean she's trying to tell me what's wrong, but she's panicked and can't give me any accurate data. I never got her interface completely set up. Be still. Don't move yourself or anything until I get her calmed down."

Tiran gives her a questioning look but remains still as she edges around him to get to the nearest bulkhead. She starts to run her hand along the smooth surface murmuring to her frightened ship. "Easy, sweetheart," she coos. "I can help, but you need to be quiet and show me where the problem is."

To her relief the alarms quiet and then shut off. The control console stops flashing every alarm, but the ship is still shaking. Mara knows her ship. Knows this type of movement means Witch is in pain. A lot of pain.

"Good, you're doing so good," she murmurs still stroking the hull. "Now light up where you need me to go."

All the lights in the room go dark except for one over the hatch to the cargo bay. "Oh no, no, no, no," she mutters and moves toward the hatch.

"Do you know of the problem now?" Tiran falls into step behind her.

"It's got to be an issue with the engine," Mara explains as she makes her way to the cargo bay hatch. Tiran follows her through the hatch and then toward the light that Witch is shining at the far end of the bay. They have to dodge around shipping containers, but soon they are both standing over a grate.

"That doesn't look good," Tiran comments as white smoke curls up in long tendrils from the grate at their feet. Mara leans forward and sniffs, recognizes the scent, and cries out in distress. She scrambles to pull open that section of flooring, sobbing in anguish when she can't get it to budge.

"Move!" Tiran commands, and she gapes up at him. Witch's distress made her forget about her passenger. He shoulders her aside and gets his fingers in the grate and strains against it. Metal shrieks and finally gives way, and Tiran staggers back holding the twisted and torn grate in his clawed hands. Before he can even throw it aside, Mara dives into the narrow space he uncovered.

"Mara, no, halt!"

She hears him call to her but ignores it. She wiggles down deeper into the area where Witch bonded with her engine components.

Most of Witch is living tissue, but like all living ships, she grew into scaffolding. Attached to that scaffolding are engines and fuel tanks. Witch can take a lot of damage from the outside, but her insides are vulnerable to heat and caustic chemicals, including the area that houses some of the engine and all the fuel lines to the engine.

Something's gone very wrong where inorganic meets organic because Mara can smell her ship's flesh burning.

The ship quakes violently around her. The pain is getting worse, and Witch is scared. "I've got you," Mara calls to her beloved ship. "I'll fix you. I'll make it all better."

Ignoring the pain in her knees as she frantically scrambles into the tight space, she follows the horrible smell of her ship's scorching tissue. She's gasping for air as she gets closer because the tight space around her is rapidly filling with toxic fumes.

Then she finds it. The same fuel feeder she

complained to Tiran about has failed again. But this time instead of just jamming, it's failed at the connection point, spraying reactive fuel all over the inside of Witch. The fuel is seeping between the crack of the non-organic area and flowing into her living tissue. It's burning Witch from the inside out.

Mara scrambles for the shut-off valve to the feeder and the fuel flow stops, but that only fixes one problem. Witch is still in immense pain from already spilled fuel.

Thinking fast, she calls back to Tiran. "Do you know what a fire suppressor bomb looks like?"

He answers without hesitation. "Yes."

"There's one in the tool chest near the hatch to the cabin. Get it, fast!" She hears him sprint off and starts wiggling backward. It seems like every other movement causes her to bang her head, elbows, or knees into something as she works her way back to the opening. The fuel fumes and smoke aren't helping her either. She doesn't have much time left before the fumes do irreparable damage. First, she'll pass out. If she isn't moved soon after passing out, the fumes will start doing the same thing to her lungs as they're doing to Witch, burning her from the inside out. It won't take long until she won't be able to breathe.

Pushing thoughts of her mortality out of her head, she focuses on saving her ship. Besides her sister, Witch is the only thing she loves. "I'm making it better," she promises the ship and then starts coughing.

"I have it," Tiran calls down to her.

Her legs are at the opening Tiran made in the deck plates. She doesn't have time to try and wiggle herself all the way out to get the fire suppressor. She flips over so she's laying on her back. "Drop it on my legs, and aim for my crotch," she orders.

Tiran hesitates. "I smell fumes, let me pull you out

and I'll go in."

"You won't fit," Mara shouts back. She knows she sounds hysterical, but she's close to panicking and doesn't have time to argue with the Hissa. "Give me the damn thing. She's in pain!"

The bomb drops and Tiran's excellent aim puts it right in the V of her legs. She grabs it, tucks it into the pocket of her suit and flips over and starts the journey back to the leak.

She's struggling with coughing fits, and her eyes are watering, making it hard to see. The discomfort only makes her push harder. Once she reaches the area where Witch is burning, she pulls the bomb out, triggers it, and then tosses it a few feet in front of her. The thing pops open and starts spewing fire suppressant chemicals. Those chemicals will make the fuel inert and act as a salve to Witch's burns.

As the bomb expands, Mara realizes she has another issue. This type of fire suppressant is designed to fill an entire cargo hull. That means it's going to keep expanding and very quickly envelop her. One of the ways this fire suppressant works is to starve a fire of oxygen. If the foam covers her, it'll do the same thing to her.

She starts wiggling backward frantically. The pain from hitting the mounting platform, ducts, and struts around her doesn't even register as she watches the foam gain on her. She tries to move faster but finds her limbs are becoming sluggish. The fumes from the fuel rob her lungs of clean air, and now the foam is going to rob her of anything to breathe.

She's going to die. She's going to die in a wave of pink foam. This was not how she expected it to happen.

I need to tell Tiran to be good to Witch, she thinks as her movements slow.

The foam is only inches from her face. She orders her limbs to move, but they don't seem to want to obey her.

Suddenly something grips her leg, and she finds herself being unceremoniously hauled backward. She grunts as she bangs into things as the iron grip around her ankle drags her out. Dazed, she blinks and watches the foam chase her through the crawl space.

With a final bang of a strut on her back, she's pulled into the cargo hold. Dangling upside down with Tiran holding one ankle, she can see his booted feet as the foam starts to emerge from the crawl space under her.

"Dumb female," he growls out as he throws her over his shoulder and sprints to the cabin. She watches the foam bursting out of the engine compartment into the cargo hold before he dives through the hatch and slams it closed behind them.

Mara feels like she's flying through the air and tries to get her body to arch so she will land on her feet, but nothing obeys her. Suddenly, the soft bunk is under her, and Tiran is looming over her again. She smiles and opens her mouth to say something but realizes she can't breathe. She gasps, trying to draw in air. Her lungs are screaming at her, and then the world around her starts fading out.

I'm sorry everybody, is the last thing she thinks before everything goes black.

CHAPTER

9

She's not breathing. Tiran would give anything to have access to a medical suite and skilled Hissa Menders. He moves to the storage compartment Mara pulled the med box from. He frantically rips the box open, breaking it apart in his haste and spilling the contents on the floor. Cursing, he grabs the scanner and rushes back to Mara's side.

He feels the ship give a little quiver, but it doesn't feel the same as before. This one is gentle, questioning. Tiran takes a guess and speaks loudly to the ship. It's hard to think of all the Space Standard words when he's this agitated, but he's able to put a few sentences together.

"She hurt but I try helping. You can help too. Help by being still so I tend to her can." He must have spoken well enough to be understood because the ship quiets, and every light in the cabin comes on at full illumination. The ship's trying to be helpful.

"Thanks," he says absently in Hissa.

Running the scanner over her chest makes it beep angrily and flash the word ERROR on the screen. With a growl of frustration, he realizes her biosuit is in the way and tosses the scanner on her legs. He grabs a hold of her suit with both hands and rips it apart, baring her body from neck to waist. Snatching the scanner back up, he curses in Hissa as he runs it over her chest again.

It gives a few beeps, then the display flashes. Her lungs are full of fuel fumes and other toxins. Tiran has no idea what to do next, but thankfully the small machine starts flashing SUGGESTED MEDICAL INTERVENTION and then a list of procedures.

He scrambles around the floor of the cabin to find the first device the scanner lists. It's a small canister with a mask attached. He holds it over her nose and mouth and hits the activation button. A short whooshing sound issues out, and he watches Mara's chest collapse as all the fumes and toxins in her lungs are pulled out. When the device flashes that it's done, Tiran pulls it away, but Mara still isn't breathing. Anxiously he looks over at the scanner screen again for what to do next. It displays both an image of the next machine and instructions.

Tiran searches the floor and finds the square machine with a face mask attachment. Snatching it up, he thrusts it against her pale face. The thing turns on the moment it touches her. He hears a whirring as it pushes air into her lungs. Her chest starts to rise and fall as the machine forces air into her.

How long should he keep it on? Will she be able to breathe on her own? What if she's permanently damaged?

It doesn't matter. He'll do everything in his power to help her. No expense will be spared to get her care. This vibrant, beautiful creature will have anything she needs. He's never used his wealth for anything other than basic necessities, the same as most Hissa men. With all the credits he's amassed, there's very little she can request that he wouldn't be able to afford. Not that she'll ask for things. It'll be up to him to find the things she needs and acquire them for her.

To his intense relief Mara starts coughing violently, her body straining against the machine's rhythm. Tiran takes it off and checks the scanner, two more steps. He's still worried but less frenzied now that she's breathing on her own.

He searches through the debris on the floor until he finds the drug the scanner recommended. She is starting to cough more brutally now, and fine particles of blood are spraying out with each forceful exhalation. He has to hold her down to inject her with the medications. In moments, the drugs are helping, and her cough quiets and stops.

The last thing the scanner tells him to do is increase her oxygen. He goes through everything in the med box but doesn't find a single thing that can do that. He looks around him, nothing. What if her brain is slowly dying because he can't get her enough oxygen?

The ship grumbles around him. A small portal next to Mara's head opens, and a little tentacle comes out, reaching over to gently touch her face. Tiran watches transfixed as it strokes her cheek and feels along her neck, then across her mouth. The ship is checking her vitals as best it can.

"Mara does well," Tiran tells Witch. The tentacle goes back to stroking her cheek. The ship grumbles around him, and the floor under him moves slightly. Startled, he steps away, but the floor keeps moving under him until he's standing next to the bunk again.

The floor stops moving, and all the lights in the ship go out except for the ones over the bunk. Witch is telling him to keep caring for Mara. He thinks about the words in Space Standard before he speaks. "You help her too. You make oxygen more in the room can? Add more oxygen for lungs to breathe?"

Nothing happens for a moment, and the tentacle disappears back into the wall. Tiran wonders if the ship can't do anything or maybe doesn't understand him. Maybe he should try asking again but this time concentrate on his Space Standard. He's worried so his words are still a mess. He should've concentrated on the language more in school, but he didn't think it was going to be that useful. He never expected to leave Hissa-controlled space.

Then he feels a breeze hit him. He looks up at the mostly dark room and can just see that several vents have appeared in the ceiling. He tastes the air. Witch is pumping in more oxygen.

Relieved, he reaches across Mara's body and strokes the

hull just like he saw Mara do. "You good ship," he tells Witch. "Mara is all proud of you." The ship makes a soft rumbling sound that makes Tiran smile. He can see why Mara was so frantic to save her ship. The two have a real bond. He finds himself slightly jealous. Is there room for one more in Mara's affections?

Mara's sleeping, and as much as Tiran wants to curl up next to her on the bunk, it's much too small to fit them both. He sinks down until he is sitting on the floor next to her. He lays his head on the bunk, close enough to her shoulder to be able to draw her wonderful smell into his lungs. He can't resist the urge to touch her, so he reaches his hand up and strokes her hair. It's only fair. She stroked his head earlier.

Making a soft, contented sound, she turns her face towards him. Her eyes never open, but she smiles in her sleep. He feels the tension in his chest finally loosen.

This woman with a warrior's spirit and a loving heart is important. He feels it deep in his chest. It's more than just wanting to bed her. He doesn't know why or how, but he's certain their fates are intertwined. She saved him in his time of need. That meant he was here to save her when Witch's fuel feed broke. She would've died in that crawl space without him present.

Whether or not she likes it, he's not leaving her side.

I don't know why the universe brought us together, he tells her silently. *But I know better than to fight fate.*

Mara wakes up slowly, giving her mind a chance to sort out all the information coming from her body. Her chest aches, but she has no problem breathing. Her skin feels tight, but she knows that sensation well; it comes from an overload of adrenaline in her system. Once she gets up and moves around the feeling of tightness will go away. It hurts a little to breathe. Her throat feels sore, and her lungs feel like she walked through a smoke-filled room. But nothing too bad.

Taking a deep breath to test her lungs, she notices the air tastes different. It takes her a moment to realize it's because there's far more oxygen content than she's used to. Why is Witch pumping in so much O2?

Opening her eyes, she finds Tiran's face so close that he's blocking out everything else. She gasps in surprise and tries to move, but he puts his massive hands on her shoulders and holds her down.

"Still!" he commands. Her fear dissolves, replaced by defiance.

"Get off!" she yells and manages to draw a leg up to kick him in the thigh. He grunts and then drops his bulk onto her, effectively pinning her to the bed.

"Be still."

Ignoring his order, she contemplates head butting him. He seems to read her intent and drops his head next to hers on the bed.

"Get off me," Mara demands and keeps struggling. He doesn't attempt to stop her struggles, just keeps her pinned and waits. Eventually she stops fighting, realizing that all he's doing is keeping her immobilized with his weight. He's not trying to tie her down or be violent to her in any other way.

When she goes still, he says something, but his words are muffled by the bedding he's hiding his face in. Hiding because he doesn't want her to hurt him.

"What? I didn't hear what you said."

Turning his face so his mouth is next to her ear, he repeats his words. "You almost die." His voice is barely above a whisper. "You stopped breathing. Please just—" His voice chokes with emotion, and he pulls in a ragged breath. His accent is getting thicker as he talks. "Just be still. Be still and let me hold you."

His words make her go still. "I stopped breathing?"

"You not get back out after set off fire suppressant bomb. I almost not reach you. I rip panel out of the floor to get you," he explains, his voice still muffled. He moves his head, nuzzling her neck with his face and breathing in deeply.

"You wedged in there *mojingla*." His warm breath caresses her skin as he talks. His accent is getting so thick he's hard to understand, and he's accidentally mixing Hissa words in with his Space Standard. "I not think I get you out. *Ulimian tosol ufayia* and then you no breathing and I was...." Tiran stops talking. "*Nilejia ewp* and I feel great fear."

The admission startles her so much that her entire body goes limp. Tiran doesn't let her up, but he moves his arms until they circle her. Then he sits up, taking her with him. He hugs her tightly to his chest and starts rocking her like a child.

Reflexively she brings her arms up to embrace him, stroking his back to comfort him. "I'm fine," she promises. She closes her eyes and sighs, letting her body relax into his hold. It's been a long time since she's touched anyone.

When his lips move against the skin of her neck to kiss her, she tenses again, and he tightens his hold. "Please not fight me," he begs. "Just let me have little taste. I sat hours. Smelling your sweet scent many hours. Only touching your hair. I just need to taste you. Just a small taste."

It doesn't seem like a good idea, but she can't seem to get her brain working well enough to tell him that. Especially after his mouth kisses her neck again, so gently it's like the flutter of an insect's wings. He nuzzles her, then kisses her again, this time with a little more pressure.

The touch of his lips sends waves of heat through her and when he grazes her neck with his sharp teeth, she gives an involuntary gasp. She feels her nipples tighten, and her heart starts to beat harder.

Inhaling deeply, he tightens his grip and runs his canines across her neck again. When he gently bites down her eyes flutter shut, and a moan escapes her.

"Give permission, little warrior," he begs her. "I not do anything else without permission."

Pulling back, she blinks open her eyes and takes in his face. The blue scale pattern is purple; his pupils are dilated so only a slight ring of color surrounds the black; and his skin feels unbelievably hot. His erection is pressing against her belly, and raw need radiates from him. But he's not rushing her. He's holding himself back and requesting approval. Knowing without a doubt he would let her go and walk away if asked, she feels powerful. Not only would he let go now if she asks, but he probably wouldn't touch her for the rest of the trip.

Understanding that makes her bold. Cupping her hand on his cheek, loving the look of desperate passion on his face, she smiles.

"Don't hurt me," she finally tells him.

"Never," he promises and lowers her back down to the bed, then sits up to look down at her chest. It's then that she realizes her biosuit is half off. It looks like it's been ripped apart, ruining it. She'll worry about it later. Right now, she needs his hands on her. She's still wearing her bra and moves to remove it, but before she can, Tiran casually rips it in half. She gives a little gasp of surprise. His wolfish grin makes her smile.

Before she can make a joke, he ducks his head down and latches onto one of her breasts. She cries out as a shock of pleasure rolls through her.

She had tried sex a few times with a crew mate many years ago. It was fast and not particularly pleasant, so she just assumed something about her DNA or the hormones they pumped into her made her unable to enjoy intercourse.

Now she thinks she's been wrong this whole time. Delightfully wrong.

"Please," she begs, but isn't sure what she's asking for.

"Shhh," he murmurs as he nuzzles against her skin. "Soon." She's glad he seems to know what she needs because she's not even sure what it is.

He lets go of her and sits up. She hates the loss of his heat, but before she can sit up and wrap her arms around him, he stands up. She watches with wide eyes as he casually tears the rest of her suit apart, flinging it away with a satisfied grunt as the ruined suit hits a far wall. He turns back to her and freezes.

Mara frowns. Has he changed his mind? He's studying her body, and she looks down at herself to find she's covered in bruises. Her stomach and breasts are about the only places not black and blue. It takes her a moment to remember her hectic movements in the engine room. Banging against everything, and then finally being brutally pulled out of the crawl space by Tiran. The whole episode left her with a lot of superficial damage. Her back is probably just as covered in bruises too.

It doesn't bother her. She's suffered much worse injuries over the course of her career in space and she barely feels pain from any of them at the moment.

She flashes a wide smile at Tiran. "I guess I'm a bit colorful right now. Don't worry, I'm a hardy soul. Now get back over here." Aggressively, she grabs one of his hands and puts it on her breast. "I want to feel more of... of whatever this is!"

Tiran blinks several times, taking in her words and her body. He seems to be having an internal dialog with himself, and then, finally, he moves. Drawing his hand out of her grip, he sinks to his knees on the bunk near her feet. She absently notices the bunk seems bigger now and wonders if Witch expanded it for them.

Then he's crawling over her, straddling her thighs but keeping all his weight on his knees. He's reaching down for her, and his hands are shaking slightly. The shocked look is gone from his face, replaced by distress.

"The scanner didn't show these," he whispers. His hands tremble a little as he touches her with infinite care, running gentle hands down the outsides of her legs.

Placing her hands over his, she pushes at them gently until they come to rest on her hipbones. She's touched by his care but has other things she'd much rather be doing than talking about bruises. "They aren't life-threatening," she explains. "And I promise, they don't hurt." Well, they don't hurt much.

Releasing one of his hands, she reaches for the prize taunting her. When her hands touch his massive cock, straining against the fabric of his suit, he makes a strangled sound. "But I'll be in some real pain if I don't get to play with this," she tells him and gives his erection a little squeeze.

His hands tighten on her hips as he draws in a lung full of air. "That feels good."

He moves a little as she strokes him through the fabric. It makes her smile with pleasure when he moans a little. She's about to sit up and see if she can get her hands into his suit to play with him when he grabs her hands and lifts them off.

"I was having fun," she pouts, and he gives a breathy chuckle.

"Me also," he admits. He leans down a little to better meet her eyes. "But healing more important than pleasure." His accent is thick again, and it takes her a moment to understand what he's saying. A soft smile stretches her mouth.

"Whatever they mixed in with the human DNA gives me a lot of advantages," she assures him. "I'm faster, stronger, age slower, and I heal faster than any other human. Just don't toss me around, and I'll be fine." She pauses, then gives him a wicked grin. "At least, don't toss me around too much." She wiggles under him suggestively, and that's all the encouragement he needs.

He releases her hands and crawls backward a bit, then reaches for her panties. She moves to raise her hips so he can slide them off, but he does the same to that fragile fabric as he did to her biosuit.

With movements bordering on violent, he rips the garment with one claw, then pulls the small scrap of fabric away from her body and tosses it aside. She expects he'll remove his suit next but instead his head dives between her legs. She isn't expecting the move and automatically tries to bring her legs together to protect herself, but his shoulders are there, wedging her legs apart and allowing him access to her sex.

"No biting!" she cries out fearfully only to hear and feel his rumbling laugh against her thighs.

"I can't promise that."

She's about to protest when his fingers slide against her. They part her lips and run the length of her labia, sending jolts of feeling as they go. He does this several times and she finds herself jerking violently every time those taunting fingers glide over her clit.

"Please!" she begs again, her voice desperate.

Gently, he works one finger into her, making her moan. Then another finger. She looks down, ready to plead with him only to see he's watching her with fierce concentration. The words die on her lips, and she can't look away. He pulls his fingers out of her and brings them to his mouth, licking her juices off each digit as if finishing a delectable meal.

"You taste unimaginably good," he tells her. All of this seems much too intense. She wants to say something sarcastic, something to break this fierce feeling of need for him. This shouldn't be so meaningful. It should just be a bit of fun, something to pass the time. Instead, a sense of wonder burns through her as if her body's been waiting for this male. Waiting for his touch and now he's here, every sensation so powerful that it overwhelms both her brain and body.

"Don't fight me."

Before she can figure out what he means by those words, he replaces his fingers with his mouth, running his tongue across her and finally latching onto her clit.

The touch causes her entire body to jerk. She screams, and her hips come off the bed, or at least they try to. He grabs her hips to hold her still because she has no control over her movements anymore. The pleasure is so intense she's panting, sweating, and bucking.

The pleasure becomes so extreme it hurts, and she wants to beg him to stop but at the same time grab his head and push him harder against her.

"More!" is all she manages to say, and he increases the pressure of his mouth.

She falls apart, her first orgasm ripping through her like an electrical shock. She can't breathe for a moment. Every muscle in her body feels locked into place as waves of pleasure course through her.

He doesn't stop until she's making a half-strangled, mewling sound. "No more," she pleads, barely able to get the words out between panting breaths.

Raising his head, he licks his lips with obvious pleasure. "You're beautiful."

No, he's the beautiful one, and she should tell him that, but doing anything more than making a contented huffing sound is outside her ability at the moment. Her body feels about as substantial as an overcooked noodle. There doesn't appear to be a single working muscle in her entire body anymore. And her brain feels about as sentient as goo. Now she knows what the female crew members were always talking about when they got so excited over hookups in port. Something like this is worth any effort or mess.

Standing up, he strips off his biosuit. He isn't wearing anything under it and his stiff cock springs free the moment the garment is out of the way. Feeling the hard length of it through the fabric of the biosuit didn't prepare her to see it standing fierce and proud. She wants to touch. Hell, she wants it in her mouth.

Eyes focused on her and his face full of lust, he kneels between her legs again. She tries to sit up so she can explore him, but he lies on top of her before she can move. His weight feels good as he settles his hips between her legs. She can feel his erection pressing against her sex and feels a moment of fear.

"It will be fine," he promises her, shifting his hips slightly so the tip of his cock is sitting just at her opening. "I'll go slow. You'll adjust." She isn't so sure about that, but before she can protest, he's easing into her. She gasps at the invasion. Her previous experiences with sex were nothing like this. It doesn't hurt as he pushes forward, there's just a sense of being full and stretched. Then he's all the way in and the base of his cock rubs her clit, making she jerks and gasps.

Breathing raggedly, he holds himself still, letting her adjust to him. "Be still, Mara," he begs. "My control is only so good."

Ignoring him, she wraps her legs around his waist, planting her heels against his muscled ass. She shifts her hips, eager for more delicious friction.

"I can't," he starts to say. Sweat is coating his body, and Mara can feel the effort it's taking him to go slow.

Moving on instinct, she wraps her arms around him, burying her face against his neck, opens her mouth, and bites down hard.

That breaks his control.

Roaring, he starts pumping into her with violent need. To her amazement it doesn't hurt. She tilts her hips so he rubs harder on her clit with each stroke, and she can feel another climax building in her.

"More," she breaths into his ear and bites him again. He gasps and rears up, breaking her hold on his shoulders. Misplaced modifier. He can move more freely in this position, so he grabs her hips to hold her still and pumps faster.

She arches against him, her back coming off the bunk as her second orgasm hits her, no less powerful than the first. She screams and is dimly aware of his cry of satisfaction echoing hers.

Gulping in air and shuddering from the pleasure, he pulls her up against him and manages to reposition both of them while remaining inside of her. He settles them back down, with him now on the bottom and her sprawled across him.

They lay there, exhausted, satiated, and unwilling to move.

This, she decides, is worth all the effort. She's never felt so relaxed in her entire life. Eventually they'll need to get up and do repairs, but at the moment all she can do is lie there, listening to the Hissa's breathing, and feeling wonderful.

"My beautiful little warrior," he murmurs to her as he strokes her back. "Sleep. I'll guard you."

"My handsome Hissa," she responds with a cheeky grin. "Sleep. I'll keep you warm." His chest shakes slightly as he chuckles.

Smiling, she snuggles into him, already half asleep as her breathing slows and her heartbeat returns to normal. She's not sure if she's ever felt so content in her life and refuses to wonder how she will go back to sleeping in the bunk by herself.

CHAPTER

11

"Why don't you go sit down and I'll do this," Tiran suggests for the tenth time since they started the repairs on Witch.

"You won't fit," Mara grunts out as she wiggles back into the compartment. It took her hours to clean out the fire suppressant foam, and she's covered in dirt, sweat, foam, and various engine lubricants. She's tired and sore, and Tiran constantly hovering over her isn't helping her mood. "Besides, I'm almost done."

Ignoring his continued grumblings, she crawls forward, pushing the new fuel feeder assembly further in front of her. She's suffered so many problems with this part over the last year that she now keeps several spares on hand for replacement. Along with Tiran's grumbling, she's also ignoring the discomfort in her own body. Her knees aren't happy at being back in the crawlspace, and she can feel every healing bruise. Her genetics mean she heals rapidly, so in a day or two there shouldn't be a mark on her, but for now she's still feeling some pain. But nothing bad enough to stop her from working. Tiran, on the other hand, has decided she's made of glass.

"What's going on? Do I need to pull you out?" he calls anxiously from above her.

"I'm fine, just moving slow," Mara tells him with an exasperated sigh. "Now stop bugging me and go play with the computer."

She hears a distinct growl of disapproval and smiles to herself. Although he's bugging the hell out of her by constantly asking how she feels or trying to get her to rest, it's nice to have someone concerned about her. It's been a long time since anyone cared about her health besides Witch.

"I don't like this," Tiran states, again.

"You don't have to like it," Mara calls and tries to keep her grin from spreading. "Just stop complaining like a frightened old man." She hears grumbling in Hissa as she slides forward.

When she's finally at the feeder assembly, she starts the tedious process of pulling the old one off and replacing it with the new one. This is one of her least favorite parts of owning her ship. She's not a skilled mechanic and always worries after a job's finished that it will fail immediately because she didn't do something right or missed a step.

Learning to do basic repairs out of necessity, she dreams of a day when she can hire someone with skills whenever she needs them. At some point she knows she'll need to employ a professional to deal with several things on Witch, and the number of credits in her account will suffer dramatically.

A major repair would be especially catastrophic now that she spent most of her savings on buying Tiran. A decision she doesn't regret but will have stark consequences in the future. It took her a long time to amass so many credits and now they're all gone.

She pushes thoughts of credits and Tiran out of her head and focuses on the task at hand. It takes effort, some cussing, and a few bloody knuckles, but she gets the part in place and secured.

With the replacement installed, she wiggles back a bit. "Fire up your fuel system," she calls out to the ship. This is the part she hates the most, starting up Witch and hoping with all her might that she did everything correctly and didn't miss any details. She needs to find a good mechanic who knows how to work on living ships.

"What?" Tiran responds anxiously.

"Not talking to you, big guy," Mara tells him with a chuckle. "I'm talking to Witch."

"That's unnerving," he grumbles, and she laughs again. Witch winds up her fuel system, and Mara watches lights come on. She holds her breath, waiting. No leaks, no blowouts, no ominous loud bangs.

"I think it's good to go. Try lighting up the engines," she calls out.

"No, you come out of there first," Tiran commands, and she can hear him trying to wedge himself in behind her.

"It's fine," she assures him. "I need to watch for leaks or other failures. I'm safe down here."

"I know for a fact you're not safe in there," he responds grimly, his accent thick with disapproval. At least he's using correct words and sentence structure. She can't see his face but can hear the scowl in his voice.

"Back off. I've got this!" she yells back at him. "Witch, fire them up."

The noise of the engines cuts off whatever he's going to say next. Mara watches the feeder carefully as pressure builds. Once she's sure it looks good, for the moment at least, she starts her journey backward. She hopes this feeder lasts. She's not eager to crawl back down here again any time soon.

The moment her legs are in view of the hatch, she feels Tiran grab her ankle and carefully start pulling her out. She relaxes her body as he draws her from the engine compartment, and eventually she's dangling in the air from one ankle. Blood rushes to her head, and a giggle escapes from her lips.

She should be annoyed at the Hissa's heavy-handed behavior but knowing it's a product of his concern more than anything else means she finds herself tolerating a lot more from him than she would anyone else.

The moment she's free from the crawl space, he grabs her waist with his other hand and flips her right side up, then lowers her onto her feet. Blood rushes out of her head, and she staggers.

"I told you this was too much work," he admonishes her

with an irritated frown. Before she can protest, he picks her up and cradles her to his chest. With long strides he weaves his way around the shipping containers and back into the cabin. He gently sets her on the bunk and starts working at the closure of her only biosuit left without any rips.

"Hold on there, handsome," she grabs his hands to stop him.

"I want to check your bruises. Be still," he commands, and Mara grins at him and lifts an eyebrow.

"Really? You just want to check my bruises?"

The scowl disappears, and a big grin spreads across his face. "And other things."

"What other things are you going to check?" Mara asks him suggestively. She can feel Witch in motion and knows the ship will resume travel to Gleem without any further instructions from her.

This is usually the part she dislikes most about doing cargo transport, the downtime between departure and arrival. Each arrival is a chance to find her sister. Each departure without finding her sister is just one more place she can cross off the list. But the downtime between arriving and leaving gives her too much time to think. Too much time to imagine all the horrible things her sister might be suffering.

The idea of spending some of that downtime cavorting with Tiran doesn't make the travel seem quite as horrible now.

Letting Tiran make quick work of her biosuit closure, she soon finds herself sprawled out under him wearing nothing but panties and a bra. He tugs thoughtfully at the bra. "Why do you wear this? It doesn't look comfortable."

Shrugging, she brushes his hand away and unclasps the garment before he can ruin it. "I wear it, so I don't swing my boobs all over the place while I move. It keeps them in check, I guess."

Giving her a decidedly hungry look, he licks his lips. "I don't mind if you swing them at me. I promise I won't move out of the way."

The laughter his words evoke is quickly turned to gasps when he runs his hands down her chest and cups both her breasts in his big powerful hands. Jolts of pleasure shoot straight down to her pussy, and she can feel herself getting wet as he starts to knead her swollen breasts, occasionally rolling the nipples between his fingers. She marvels at the size of his hands as they move on her flesh. The man is just massive everywhere.

"You're so perfect," he murmurs to her.

"Even if I'm kind of small?" she asks, surprised at her insecurity. Tiran regards her curiously.

"We fit together perfectly. You aren't too small," he points out, and she blushes a little.

"That's not what I meant," she tells him quickly, then squirms when he pinches one of her nipples between his thumb and finger a little harder than previously.

"What did you mean, little warrior?" he asks as he brings his face down to nuzzle at her neck and shoulder.

"I looked up Hissa on the computer while you were asleep," she tells him. "It didn't have much information, and we were too far away from a station to connect to any big network, but there were pictures. Your women are as big as you."

Her words make him draw in a sharp breath and rear back. He's looking down at her with a surprised expression. Then he pulls his hands away from her, and she wonders what's wrong, but before she can ask, his face takes on a mournful expression. "Yes, it's true our women were tall," he tells her.

"Were?"

"There was an illness," he tells her bluntly, his face bleak.

"Yes, I know, I read about that." Her voice is soft.

"But you don't know how devastating it was. We kept that a secret. When I was a boy, it killed my mother. It killed all the Hissa women. It devastated our male population too. We found a vaccine against it but much too late."

"All the women?" She's astonished. She knew the Hissa suffered a terrible loss of life due to disease but didn't know that all the women had died. No wonder the guy looks so upset. The outlook for a species with no females is a dismal one. Sitting up, she wraps her arms around him. He accepts her embrace with a sigh, and she can feel him relax into her.

"All." He manages to pack a lot of sadness and desolation into that one little word.

"But how…" she lets her sentence trail off. He doesn't need her to state the obvious.

The sound he makes breaks her heart. It's part resignation and part frustration. "We're trying to find the answer to our problem, but so far our efforts have been fruitless."

"What about the science that created me and my sister?"

"We tried the human Decanting technology, but none of the infants survived. We can't be grown in vats."

"What about compatible species? Can you get any other race pregnant? They wouldn't be pure Hissa children, but half is better than none."

"We'd be fine with half-breed children. Our males would love and care for the mothers of their children even if they weren't Hissa, but so far we haven't found a species that's breeding compatible," Tiran confesses. There's a moment of silence, and then he speaks so softly she can barely hear him. "We're losing hope."

For the first time, she realizes how dire the Hissa plight is. Hugging him tightly, she wishes there was some way she could help. They sit like that, entwined and drawing comfort from each other until one of her legs starts falling asleep. She tries to move it without upsetting their embrace and manages to push herself against his massive erection.

She pulls away just far enough to meet his gaze. His face is a strange combination of lust and guilt. She decides she wants passion to take over his expression and push the guilt and sadness away.

Patting his hardening cock, she grins. "Is that for me?"

Barking out a laugh, he hugs her tightly. She lets him hold her like that for a little while, then wiggles until he releases her. Eagerly, she starts undoing his biosuit. "Let's make the playing field a little more even."

Hands coming up to help her, she makes an impatient sound and bats them away, "Let me open my present. You just stand up and keep looking gorgeous."

Grinning, he obediently stands to allow her access to all the suit closures. She takes her time, kissing and touching each inch of flesh she reveals as she peels the suit away. Every muscle on him is tense and the sounds he's making tell her he's both enjoying himself and feeling rather tortured.

When she gets to his ass, she pauses to admire one of her favorite parts of his anatomy. The muscles under her hand tremble a little as if begging to be touched. But she's in the mood for a little taunting.

Squeezing, she enjoys the half choking, half growling noise he makes, then she leans in and gives him a little nip. Only one pant leg of his suit is still on and with a fluid motion he kicks it off, turns and grabs Mara. She finds herself flat on her back on the bunk in a blur of motion.

"No," she protests, trying to pull away. "I wanted to do that to you first."

"Later," he growls and grabs her thighs in an iron grip. "I need the taste of you in my mouth." He pulls her legs apart and dives at her, making her flinch from the barely controlled aggression. Then his lips are on her, tongue lapping at her sex, and she can't do anything but pant and gasp.

This isn't the patient, carefully controlled lover of before. This man is in deep need, and the way he uses his mouth with force just shy of pain makes her buck under him. Half of her wants to get away; half of her wants to push against him harder.

All of her is enjoying the ride. "Oh, fuck!"

Startled, he pops his head up and looks at her. "Did I hurt you?"

"No, no," she assures him between ragged breaths. "It's just, the thing. The thing you just did. That felt..." She can't find the words, and Tiran smiles at her.

"You like it," he declares with triumph. She wants to ask him to slow down. To ease up a bit. Everything she's feeling is too intense, too new. But no words come out, and she screams again when he latches on, this time bringing his fingers into play. Just like with his mouth, his fingers are rougher this time, but the harshness only makes it better.

As the pleasure gets more intense, she tries to wiggle away from him, sure she can't take any more. He clamps one hand down on her. That possessive hand holding her still puts her over the edge. She's so out of breath when she climaxes that she can't even scream. Instead, her upper body rears off the bed, the pleasure so intense all her muscles seem locked in place. Spots appear in her vision, and she can't seem to draw enough air into her lungs.

When he finally pulls his mouth away, she slumps back on the bed, hoping he's not going to ask her to move for at least a few days. Or weeks.

"My turn," he says, and she feels guilty. She's not sure she can make herself move well enough to go down on him.

"I can't," she starts, but he hushes her with a kiss and moves to cover her with his body. She can taste herself on his lips and finds she likes it.

"Hush, sweet warrior," he murmurs to her, his body sweating and quaking slightly. "Let me have this with no resistance."

He moves his hips between her legs. He reaches down, and she can feel him guiding himself inside her. The first stroke is slow and deliberate, and she sighs with the delicate pleasure of it.

She wraps her legs around his hips and her arms around his chest and draws him to her, gasping a little as it causes her clit to rub harder against him. He becomes perfectly still, and she wonders if she's hurting him somehow.

"I want to go slow," he grinds out, his voice tense and strained. "I want to be gentle to you. I want to give you more pleasure, but I'm on edge. I'm worried about hurting you. I don't want to go too fast."

Willing to go along on any ride with him, she manages to get a hand up to pat his chest. "It was good last time. Do that again."

Ignoring her, he rears back and pulls out of her.

"No!" she starts to protest, but she doesn't have a chance to get any more words out. He grasps her around the waist and flips her over. A little dazed by the move, she gives a soft cry of surprise when he grabs her hips and pulls her up on all fours.

Leaning over her, he pushes until only the head of him is inside her. Then the bastard stops moving.

"Now you can make sure it feels good," he tells her. Looking over her shoulder to meet his gaze while she reprimands him for moving her around like a rag doll, she accidentally pushes him a little further inside her. Both of them give a little groan.

Experimentally, she pushes back some more until he's fully seated in her. She collapses her shoulders down to the bed and moves a few times, slowly moving back and forth on his erection, enjoying the feeling. Then he reaches his hand around and pinches her clit with his fingers. The bundle of nerves, already sensitive from her first orgasm, sends a shock of sensation through her.

"More!" she demands, moving on his dick with more ferocity now. He alternates between pinching and rubbing as she starts pushing violently against him. She's so close to another orgasm. It's looming just out of her reach.

Whimpering with need, she becomes a little more frantic. In response, he increases the pressure of his fingers and helps her by thrusting his hips into hers, seating himself even deeper inside. The sound of flesh smacking flesh fills the cabin as their wild movements send both of them over the edge.

Just as her orgasm takes her breath away and sweeps her legs out from under her, he roars and crashes down, sending them both sprawling onto the bed. Gasping for breath, he rolls over, taking her with him and keeping their bodies connected. He's shuddering and gulping air, making her grin with pride. She enjoys reducing her big Hissa into a panting, shaking mess.

They lay like that, their heartbeats gradually slowing and their breathing evening out. She shivers a little as the sweat dries on her skin and wonders if she has the energy for a shower. She feels sated and sleepy, maybe a nap then a trip to the cleansing unit.

"I can't imagine my life without you," he whispers in her ear, making her tense up. She's wide awake now.

He sounds serious, and she's not sure how she feels about it. Caring for others is dangerous. This is supposed to be about fun until she gets Tiran to a place where he can take care of himself. This isn't supposed to be about commitment or longevity. Suddenly she needs some space.

Tapping his shoulder, she clears her throat and tries to sound nonchalant as she speaks. "Cuddle time has been fun, but we have stuff to do. I need you to let go of me now."

Shaking his head, he gently pulls his softening cock free of her, then urges her to lay on her back. Once she rolls over, he throws one heavy leg over both of hers and curls one large arm around her chest just under her breasts.

"I'm sorry I spoke," he tells her quickly. "I didn't mean to make you feel uncomfortable. Forget my careless words. Just lay with me for now."

Torn between wanting to get away from him and wanting to cling, she remains still and wars with herself for a moment. What can it hurt to cuddle for a bit? He's probably feeling emotional from their discussion earlier about the lack of Hissa women and needs comfort. She's not so cruel as to pull away from him now.

There'll be plenty of time to set him straight about their relationship, or lack thereof, later. Settling back against him, she closes her eyes and strokes his chest, soothing both of them. He gives a small, contented sound, and she smiles.

"Thank you," he murmurs to her.

"Don't get used to it," she warns him.

He's silent for a long time, and she's on the verge of sleep when he speaks again, his voice so sorrowful it makes her heart hurt. "I'll try not to."

CHAPTER 12

Looking up from her spot on the floor, Mara watches Tiran glower at her control console. Well, not the entire control console, just the one part of it that he's holding in his big hands. His scale pattern is a dark brown, a sure sign of irritation. He notices her looking at him and gives a low sound of frustration, flashing a hint of fang.

Damn, she loves those fangs.

"Whoever did this should be pushed out an airlock," he growls, holding up a part of her control console. The guts of the console are all spread out around him. The careful way he took it apart and placed everything tells her there's an order to the chaos. But to her it looks like a small beast burrowed into her ship and tossed everything out to make room for a nest.

"Is that going to go back together?" she asks with concern. "It's impossible for Witch to control her engines if that thing isn't in place."

"I'll get it back together, but it's junk," he tells her, waving the small part violently. "It's installed incorrectly, and it's missing vital components. I'm amazed Witch is doing as well as she is considering the poor work done on her." He looks down at the mess around him and picks up another part and holds it up for her to see. "This should have at least three more leads. Look at it! There are only two! Two!" She nods emphatically at his words even though she has no idea what he's holding.

"Only two is bad?"

"It's probably why the feeders keep jamming. She doesn't have enough command avenues to create pressure settings so it's all or nothing on the feeder. They jam because she can't throttle back."

Realization dawns on Mara. "She doesn't have enough lines of communication with the engine."

"Yes, like that," Tiran grunts and then points to the part of the console he's disassembled. "This is all badly done."

"I didn't have the money for a professional," she admits, feeling inordinately guilty. She strokes the floor next to her. "I'm sorry, Witch. I didn't know it was so bad."

"I can fix it," Tiran tells her, his voice now gentle. He eyes the console. "For now, I will put it back together as before and just work with the programming to make better use of what little is here. Once I can get the parts, I can rework the entire thing and improve it for Witch."

"How expensive are the parts?" she asks anxiously. She wants Witch to have the best, but there is little in the way of credits in her account, and she needs enough at the next station to buy fuel and other essentials before she can consider spending on anything else.

"Expensive. You need dimmerion components, or Witch will find it hard to interface."

Shaking her head, she tosses her long hair over her shoulder. "There's no way I can afford all dimmerion parts. It's the most expensive stuff on the market." Stroking Witch, she murmurs, "I promise I'll get as much as I can as soon as I can." Even though she knows with the console down the ship can't hear her.

After a long burn, Witch shuts the engines down, coasting to their destination in order to conserve fuel. It's all standard procedure, so Tiran decided to take advantage of the downtime and tinker, as he put it.

Mara would say a better description might be destroy, not tinker.

Going back to fiddling with items that seem far too small for his large hands to handle, he mutters something about stupid people using the wrong parts. She watches him for a few minutes and decides not to take anything he's saying personally. He's in his element and used to working with superior materials. It's a new side of Tiran she hasn't seen before, but it doesn't bother her. It's cute that he's affronted on behalf of her ship.

But that's only half the new behavior he's displaying. He seems to be ignoring her. Except for brief interactions about the ship, he's ignored her the entire day. Considering the marathon-like sex from the days before, it's a drastic change, and Mara finds it not only unsettling, but also hurtful.

It started that morning. Tiran woke first and got out of the bunk immediately without trying to wake her or initiate sex. He proceeded to get right to work, ripping her console apart and pretending Mara wasn't there unless he needed a question answered.

She might've been the one reluctant to enter any kind of formal relationship, but it's still painful to have Tiran just shut her out like that. In less than a day she'll be dropping him off at Gleem and picking up another cargo contract. She's determined to say goodbye to the big Hissa without regret. She'll always treasure the time they've shared, but they both have missions to continue. He needs to find a solution for his people, and she needs to find her sister.

Maybe someday, after she's got Lara back, she'll visit the Hissa homeworld. From the brief entry in her database about Tiran's home planet, the place is lush with life with an atmosphere compatible to humans. Perhaps she and Tiran can pick up where they left off.

If he wants her to visit, that is. Considering his current mood, she's not sure he even wants to speak with her before they part ways on Gleem.

Shrugging her shoulders, she tries not to dwell on their imminent parting. She's got contract requests to put together and that absorbs her until she hears a distant ding. She looks up from the small holographic display she's been using to find Tiran standing over the control console, taping one of the displays. It's all back together, but he doesn't look happy.

"Is it working?"

"Of course, it is," he tells her in a sullen tone. "Did you think I would break it?"

That's it. She's had enough of his attitude. "You're acting like I stole your favorite blanket. I don't know what's going on, but you need to stop with the weird mood," she commands. "Whatever's bothering you, work it out. I don't deserve your attitude."

Expecting a confrontation, almost eager for it, she's left reeling when he doesn't get mad. His shoulders slump a little, and his expression turns depressed. He drops his gaze and sighs softly. "I apologize. I'm nervous about the future."

Then it hits her. She picked him up as a fluke, a slave to free, a good deed done. But to him, the last few days were filled with apprehension, fear, and distress. Even though they combed through the news feeds, they couldn't find out what happened to his ship or his crew mates. With no idea if they're even alive, or what will happen to his mission and people now, he's got the right to be a little moody. Hell, in his position she'd be in such a foul mood she'd be banging on anything handy.

That gives her an idea.

"I think we need a distraction. Let's have some fun," she chirps with forced cheer.

Looking up, he raises his browridge in suspicion. "This distraction doesn't have anything to do with airlocks and my dead body, does it?"

Laughing, she shakes her head. "No, I mean, let's do some training. Maybe sex later if you're done being an asshole."

With an eager nod, he steps back to give her room to stand up and stretch. "Training sounds good. I'm agitated. I'd like some physical exertion. And sex is good exertion too. Yes. I say yes to both of them."

"Witch, bring out the trainers," she calls out, trying to

control her laughter at Tiran's puppy-like enthusiasm. Six tentacles appear from the ceiling in a circle and Mara moves to stand among them. She settles herself in a fighting stance and then calls out, "Begin."

The tentacles start moving, slowly at first but gaining speed as time continues. Mara ducks, weaves, jumps, and rolls to avoid the tentacles. She punches one, kicks another, and elbows a third. As the speed of the exercise increases the tentacles narrow, making it harder to see or hit them. Eventually one of the tentacles knocks her down with a leg sweep she couldn't quite avoid. She lays on the floor, panting and laughing. One of the tentacles reaches down and hovers just above her.

Grasping the appendage, she uses it to get to her feet. Once she's standing again all the tentacles go still, waiting for orders.

"Nice," she calls out to Witch. "That was just perfect." All the appendages give a little wave of pleasure then go still again.

She looks over to see Tiran gaping at her. "You do this often?"

Proud of the training regimen she and Witch developed over the years, she gives him a big grin as she rolls her shoulders. "All the time. Keeps me in shape, and Witch sees it as a kind of game. I get to practice; Witch gets to help me practice and see improvement. That makes her happy when I get better."

Closing his mouth with an audible click, his expression moves from shock to disapproval. "She could hurt you!"

Smile gone; she regards him coldly. "That could happen. She could even kill me if she wanted to, but she won't. We're partners."

Moving between her and the training circle, he glowers. "This isn't safe. You shouldn't do this."

Done with both this conversation and his attitude, Mara crosses her arms under her breasts and glares at Tiran. "You know what isn't safe? Leaving my ship. Every time I walk out that hatch, I'm in danger. I'm one of the few cargo transporters that's by myself. No crew or backup. The only way to make sure I'm safe is to be prepared. If I could, I'd just carry weapons, but as you know, most stations have the scanners so you can't make it off the docks with any kind of weapon. That means my body needs to be the weapon, and this is how I prepare. And this is also one of the ways Witch and I keep ourselves entertained on long trips." She jabs a finger in his direction to emphasize her next words. "Besides, I don't remember asking for your opinion."

The dark, forbidding expression on his face diminishes as she talks. The blank in his scale pattern lightens to blue, and real regret shows on his face. He's looking at this training in a different light now.

"Again, I'm sorry. I wasn't thinking of the troubles you face on your own." Turning back to the training circle, he regards the tentacles thoughtfully. "Does it hurt Witch when you hit these?"

Huffing out a breath and feeling a little dizzy from the speed of Tiran's mood swings, she shakes her head. "No. If I used a plasma torch it would hurt her, but there's nothing I could do with my body that could damage her."

With a decisive nod, Tiran moves into the circle of tentacles. "I wish to try."

"Of course, that was the whole point of this, so you could try it too. Just call out 'begin' when you're ready. Call out 'end' if you want her to stop before you're on the ground. It's cheating if you leave the circle. She wins when your back lands flat on the ground. She won't grab you around the middle or the throat."

"Understood," Tiran says, looking around him carefully, gauging Witch and his space. Then he puts himself in an aggressive fighting stance and calls out, "Begin."

Witch treats Tiran just like Mara, moving, grabbing at limbs, and trying to trip him to the floor. Just like Mara, he easily avoids them, and lands blows on the tentacles as they move around him. Witch increases the speed gradually and soon Tiran is almost matching Mara's speed.

When his big body hits the floor, the impact is enough for Mara to feel it through her own feet as the flooring shakes a little. With him on his back, the tentacles go still. He lasted a lot longer than she expected, considering his size is a disadvantage in this game.

He barely takes long enough to draw in a lung full of air before he's flipping himself back on his feet.

"That—" she starts, but his roar interrupts her.

"Begin!"

Witch hesitates. She isn't used to roaring, but when Tiran remains within the tentacles, she begins again. Mara watches Tiran closely. He conserves his movements at first, just tapping the tentacles instead of putting real force behind his blows. As the speed increases, he makes his movements more forceful and violent. Soon he's all motion, and Witch is moving so fast Mara doesn't even see the blow that lands him on his back.

Getting to his feet a little more slowly this time, his chest is rising and falling rapidly to accommodate his ragged breathing.

Mara steps forward. "That was well done—" she starts to say, but he cuts her off with a glower.

He rolls his head, then shoulders, as if testing for breaks or injuries, then lowers himself back into stance. "Begin!" he barks out.

Filled with admiration, she watches Tiran move, thoroughly impressed by the Hissa's endurance. His accuracy and speed are barely compromised by fatigue. But even with his speed and endurance, Witch knocks him down.

Remaining silent, she waits to see what he'll do. He rolls over on his side and then gets on all fours, breathing hard and sweating enough to leave an outline of his body on the floor. He shakes his head, sits back on his heels, and then pops up on his feet. He puts up his fists and calls out, "Begin."

This time he only lasts half as long. He's winded, and Mara can tell by the way he slowly gets up that he's hurting. Before he can call out to Witch, Mara ends the exercise. "Exercise over, retract, Witch." The tentacles disappear back into the ceiling, and Tiran looks over at her accusingly.

"Bring those back. I'm not done."

"You're bleeding," Mara tells him tartly. "That means playtime is over."

"I'm not done!" He roars, and Mara has to force herself not to take a step back. There's something different about Tiran at the moment. He seems almost feral. She wonders what's going on in his head.

"I'm captain of this ship," she states flatly and enunciates each word with force, so he doesn't mistake her meaning. "And you aren't even crew. You will not give me orders on my ship." She points to the small bathroom. "Go shower and cool off. Roar once more and I'll have Witch restrain you. And she's not nice when she does that." It's a bluff. Witch doesn't know how to restrain anyone. At least not yet. But once she's finished on Gleem, she's going to make damn sure that gets integrated into their training from this point on.

Stiffening, his expression goes from aggressive to concerned in the blink of an eye. "I wouldn't attack you."

"Well, you could've fooled me," Mara retorts. "You've been in a foul mood all day, and I thought we were getting along great. My mistake. Take a shower, and I'll go hang out in the cargo hold for the next few hours. That way you don't need to be anywhere near me. Once we get to Gleem you can be out the hatch and gone. I'll just be an unpleasant memory."

Turning to leave, she stops when a gentle hand lands on her shoulder. Turning back, she glares at him. "Looking to fight me now that you can't play with Witch anymore?"

"No, I don't wish to fight you at all. That's why I took advantage of your practice circle. But I couldn't win. I failed, even though you allowed me several attempts."

She relaxes a bit. Maybe his male pride is punctured. "Look, no one can beat the game. It's a training exercise. If we could beat it, then it wouldn't help us be better fighters."

"You beat me." The words don't have any emotion to them, but the set of his face and shoulders tells her he's struggling to come to terms with the outcome of their battle when he first boarded Witch.

"I'm really good," is the only thing she thinks to say and when his shoulders slump, she feels horrible. She wouldn't like to be beaten either. "It was close," she adds truthfully, hoping that helps. "You're a really good fighter."

"I wanted to show you I'm strong," he says and looks down at his bloody knuckles. "I thought I would be better than you at this exercise. I wanted to show you I'm a warrior, but perhaps I'm not."

"You did well. People usually get dumped on their ass a lot faster," she tells him quickly. "I think you lasted a little longer than me that first time. I promise I'm impressed."

"You are?" He looks like she just told him he was king of the universe.

"I am," she nods her head emphatically. "And I know you have more stamina than I do. I can only do two rounds at best. I've never even thought of trying four rounds in a row. That's my weakness, endurance. I have an issue. Both of us, me and my sister Lara have the same issue. When our adrenaline spikes, we don't have long before we pass out. I don't know if we were designed that way or it's a flaw they didn't realize. But I envy you."

Back straightening, a gratified smile forms on his face. "I do have excellent endurance."

Returning his smile with one of her own she nods again. "Yes, you're very resilient." She hopes she's hit on the reason for his foul mood. She can relate to feeling low because an opponent beat you. What does surprise her though, is the fact that it took so long for the incident to bother him. It happened days ago. Why is he getting upset now?

"I wanted to prove that to you." He takes a small step towards her.

She eyes him warily. She's not sure she trusts this new mood, considering how churlish he's been. "Prove what?"

"That I could beat you."

Taking a quick step back she brings up her fists, ready to defend if he decides to suddenly become violent. "What do you mean?"

Tiran holds up his hands quickly. "I won't strike you."

Dropping to the floor in one fluid motion, he sits down hard on his ass and stretches his legs out in front of him. He puts his big hands behind his neck and laces his fingers together. She gapes at the extremely vulnerable position he just put himself in.

"I'm no threat." His expression is earnest, and his words are spoken softly. "I would never hurt you."

Sinking to her knees in front of him and feeling thoroughly confused, she puts a hand on his shoulder and kneads her fingers gently into his muscles. "Let's back up here a bit. Why's it so important I see that you can fight?"

"I needed to prove to you that I'm a worthy male." His words make her eyes drop to his crotch involuntarily, and she hears him chuckle. Blushing, she looks back up.

"There are more ways than one to be a worthy male," he tells her.

"I guess I find you worthy all over the place, or we wouldn't have spent so much time naked."

A small frown mars his features. "But I need you to know I can protect you."

Flopping back on her butt, she joins him on the floor and gives him a little shake of her head. "We've been over this before big guy. I don't need you to protect me. I'm doing great."

"I disagree. You even pointed out how dangerous it is every time you need to dock and leave the ship. I needed to show you that despite our first interaction on board Witch, I'm a capable protector. I was struggling with how to show you this without having to fight you again. Witch provided me with a means to prove myself to you, but it didn't go as well as I hoped."

His little speech raises more questions than it answers, but their conversation is put on hold when a ding sounds and Witch fires up her engines.

A wave of misery goes through her. Any conversation with Tiran isn't just on hold: it's effectively over. They are almost to Gleem, and she's going to have to say goodbye.

"We're about to dock. Time to get cleaned up," she forces her voice to be cheerful and light. "Looks like we'll be on Gleem soon."

Frowning, he slowly gets to his feet. "I'll ready myself to accompany you on the station. I've heard of Gleem. It's not a very lawful place."

It's true. Gleem is one of the more disreputable stations but not any worse than most of the ones she visits. She doesn't need an escort, but he might as well go with her. Once she finishes signing off on the cargo, she can walk Tiran around until they find him a transport to his homeworld or a job.

And I won't cry when we part, she states firmly. She's pretty sure she's lying.

Tiran watches Mara with admiration as she negotiates with the Fozin merchant called Tifle. It's obvious she's well versed in these types of transactions because she doesn't let the little furry Fozin intimidate her with station security, his family, or the two goons standing silently behind him. She remains firm, and he ungraciously gives in.

"You're an unrepentant thief," Tifle tells her as he holds out his data bracelet for her to scan. "I will tell everyone what a thief you are, and no one will work with you again."

"I'm the only one you could get to haul for you," Mara replies with a bland expression. "Say what you like. Everyone knows you're impossible to deal with. Even other Fozin don't like to do business with you."

Suddenly the little merchant's eyes narrow, and he regards Mara shrewdly. "My brother, Neff, met you when you were attending a slave auction. He made me aware that there are credits to be had. That means I've another deal to broker with you. It'll be beneficial for both of us. I've done extensive negotiations, and you will be very pleased."

Mara's expression doesn't change. "What deal?"

The Fozin grins, showing rows of crooked needle-like teeth. In the center of his teeth gleams a fang, probably polished to be brighter than the rest. The length and brightness of that center fang is considered a sign of beauty. Tifle's fang is so long it rests on his lower lip. He probably had it surgically enhanced. It would look better if the rest of his needle teeth weren't dark with rot.

"There is someone interested in acquiring a human woman. The contract has clauses to protect you," he chitters with excitement, "the price is rather high for an alien as ugly as you. There's no reason not to accept."

To Tiran's surprise Mara doesn't get upset. She just rolls her eyes and taps a few things on her data bracelet to finish the transaction. "Yup, heard that before and I'm still not interested."

Making an upset, chittering noise, Tifle waves his hands in the air as if to brush away her negative reaction. "But he's willing to pay a hundred credits for a contract with you! He could buy several slaves with no contract for that."

Looking mildly annoyed now, she frowns at the Fozin. "I bet it's more like three hundred, and I'm still not interested."

Grabbing her with a little paw, he digs small claws into her forearm. "No, you must," he hisses at her in panic. "You must. I've already accepted the deal. I'll give you the entire four hundred, but you must agree."

Clutching his hands into fists to keep from stepping in and throwing the little creature away from her, Tiran glares at the furry merchant. His intervention is entirely unnecessary because Mara makes quick work of the annoying Fozin.

With one hand, she reaches down and unhooks his little claws from her arm, then tosses him at one of his enormous bodyguards. The guard catches Tifle and carefully sets him down without a change of expression. Making loud, sharp, angry noises, Tifle stomps one little foot, then motions and the guards take a step forward. But the guards hesitate when Mara clears her throat and points up. Tifle, Tiran, and the guards all look up to regard the security feeds all around them.

"I could easily call station security," she points out and the expressions on the guards' faces turn worried. "Don't try me. I know they've been wanting to get their hands on you for a while."

It's one thing to threaten but to touch her without permission would get him tossed off the station. At least here there are security cameras watching and a program is monitoring the feed ready to alert station security to any violence or illegal activity. Although Gleem doesn't have the best reputation, order still needs to be maintained in the common areas.

"Stupid, stupid, stupid female," Tifle curses her, waving his guards back.

"I'm not the one who sold a product he didn't own," Mara points out blandly.

"Worthless female. Weak, clawless human. I know you were a slave. I know you're Decanted. The scars never lie. Born to be a slave. You should be falling to your knees to fulfill this contract and your purpose."

The insults don't appear to bother her, but Tiran hasn't spent his adult life being insulted, and he is angry on her behalf. He tenses next to her and starts to move forward, but a gentle hand on his arm stops him.

"It's not worth it to fight those guys. I've gotten into scuffles with them before. They have hard heads." She grins at him and mimics shaking her hand out. "Makes your knuckles hurt."

Tiran gives her a small smile but doesn't relax. He doesn't trust this merchant.

"Are we done?" he asks Mara, anxious to leave the small, odious Fozin behind.

Tifle is making angry sounds and talking into his personal com. Tiran assumes he's trying to get the money together to pay back whoever was willing to pay so many credits for a contract with a human without even seeing her first. Mara should be more concerned about this unknown buyer with so many credits to burn. She's much too indifferent for his liking. The sooner he gets them both back on Witch, the happier he'll be.

She nods. "All done. Just need to hit the market area and then we can find you transport. I made enough off this that I should be able to get you passage all the way to Hissa."

That hurts. She's so eager to send him away. He must not have proven himself a worthy male for her yet. Her lack of enthusiasm to keep him can't be a lack of pleasure. He knows she enjoys his body. Her responses to him can't be a lie.

Before the Great Death, competitions were always being held so men could show off their prowess in mock battle or with feats of speed, strength, or ingenuity. And yet, here he is with no wealth and not even sure what happened to his ship and crew. To make matters worse, their first meeting was at a slave auction. Not only did she purchase him, but she won their confrontation later that day. Despite everything she said about admiring his endurance, he's positive his training session with Witch didn't help raise his value in her eyes.

Could she still be harboring contempt for him? Does she see him as an unworthy male?

Shame fills him as he contemplates all his failures.

No! he refuses to be defeated. She might not see him as worthy now, but he'll figure out a way to leave this station with her and convince her that he's deserving of her esteem. Eventually, he'll need to return to Hissa, but he doesn't want to make that journey unless Mara is with him. That means he needs time with her. Time to convince her of his value. Time to convince her to stay with him.

He's thinking so intently on how to get her to let him stay on Witch that he doesn't realize she's talking to him. "What?"

"Where did you go?" she teases him. They stop and face each other. They're standing at one end of the market area's thoroughfare. "Your body was here, but your mind was someplace entirely different." Suddenly she sobers, all humor vanishing. "Are you scared to go home? I know you're worried about being an outcast because you were sold into slavery, and you couldn't finish your mission. But I can promise that no one knows what happened."

Keeping the wince off his face takes effort as she reminds him of all the lies he told her to get sympathy. At some point he's going to need to tell her the truth, but not right now. Revealing his duplicity isn't going to win him a spot on Witch and at Mara's side.

"I'm concerned," he states carefully. It's somewhat the truth. He is concerned about their future.

Biting her lip, she walks him further along the thoroughfare, now deep in her thoughts. She seems to come to some decision because she looks up and gives him a brilliant smile.

"I could send you home with testimony that I found you. We could just skip the whole slavery and auction part. You don't even need to pay me back, so you can just forget about it. If no money needs to be exchanged there's no trail. It can be like it never happened. At least as far as record-keeping goes."

He's annoyed both at himself for telling the Dishonored lie in the first place and at her for being so focused on it. And now she's trying to tell him he doesn't even owe her credits. He's seen the state of her finances after working on Witch's control console.

He scowls darkly at her. "I won't forget about it. You spent your savings on me. I was a slave, and now I stand free, not because of any effort or bravery on my part but because of your charity."

Throwing up her hands, she scowls right back at him. "Fine, go ahead and dig that honor grave for yourself. I hope it's comfortable."

She stalks off, leaving him confused. It takes him a moment to realize he was thinking about the money he owes her for his purchase, but she's still focused on solving his "Dishonor" problem.

Cursing at himself in Hissa, he tries to think of ways he can show her that he's valuable as a companion as he hurries after her. Catching up in just a few strides, he walks with her in silence for a moment before trying again.

"I meant I won't forget about how you helped me. You're not wealthy, and you spent credits to buy me. And to clothe me for space travel. I was just trying to tell you I appreciate it."

Stopping and facing him, she rolls her shoulders as if trying to dispel tension and gives him a tentative smile. "Sorry, I guess you're not the only one on edge. Let's see what we can find here for Witch and then we'll look at passenger contracts for you. And I need to check to see if anyone picked up one of my cargo contracts."

Eager to improve life for her and Witch, he looks around at the shops surrounding them. Gleem isn't a big station, so the selection is scanty. "There won't be any dimmerion here, but a hybrid would work. I can swap it out quickly without the systems needing to be down for very long."

"If you show me what to buy, I might be able to do it myself." Her suggestion makes him scowl.

Oh no, he doesn't like that idea. No one else should be putting their hands on Witch's computer components except him, not even Mara herself. He's sure if Witch could talk, she would agree with him. For now, he ignores her suggestion and nods his head to a display table standing just outside a small, crowded shop.

"That place looks like it might have what we want." It looked to be full of secondhand components, but even a used half-dimmerion part is better than what Witch is dealing with now.

They meander over and Mara starts chatting with the merchant while Tiran digs through the parts, almost giving a triumphant little shout when he finds what he needs. They bargain and Mara does her best, but in the end, she can't get the merchant to drop the price enough for her to afford the part.

Tiran feels immense frustration as he puts the part back in the
bin but manages to keep his emotions in check.

The Hissa are a rich species with a small population.
With his personal resources he could easily buy Witch an entire
new console made of pure dimmerion instead of trying to
bargain for one used part that's only made up of half
dimmerion. But he possesses no data bracelet, so he can't access
any of his funds. They could send a communication to Hissa,
but Witch doesn't have a powerful enough array to receive the
reply that would come days later. Trying to buy message time
on the station array would be prohibitively expensive.

Determined to make it up to her as soon as he's able, he
throws a consoling arm around her shoulders and draws her
against him as they walk away from the shop. Looking let
down, she leans into him and sighs.

"You got me all excited about new parts for Witch." The
disappointment in her voice makes his chest hurt. Other females
might be interested in clothing, exotic jewels, or fancy
furnishing, but not his Mara. No, she wants her living ship to be
happy.

"I'm sorry, little warrior," he says as he hugs her. "It
wasn't a particularly good part anyway. I would've needed to
replace it within a Space Standard year." She chuckles at his
words and hugs him back.

"It's fine. I just feel bad for Witch," she gives another
little sigh. "One day I'll figure out how to get her the good stuff.
For now, I guess we can both just make do."

He wants to tell her that she doesn't have to "make do."
He can provide her with everything she needs but knows that's
not what she wants to hear. Mara isn't one to sit back and let the
universe just fall into place around her. No, she's a fighter. She
possesses the kind of will that refuses to bend. It's one of the
things he finds most wonderful and frightening about her. She's
got the spirit of a Hissa to match her warrior grace.

The one thing she wants more than anything is to find
her sister Lara and he's determined to make that happen. If she

can be found, that is. She might be dead, buried in an unmarked grave on some planet or moon. Mara might spend her life searching and never find her. Despite that dismal thought, he's still willing to search the universe alongside Mara. All he'll need to do first is talk her into visiting Hissa so he can check in with his people and get access to his wealth.

Is that all he needs? Could he be happy in space, away from Hissa and everything he's familiar with?

It's the first time he's thought about it. He likes space travel, and he's a skilled programmer and computer engineer. He could spend years fine tuning Witch's computers and perhaps sell the finished program to other living ship owners.

The thought doesn't bother him. The idea of being cooped up in a small space with Mara for the rest of his life makes him feel a strange kind of anticipation. Maybe he could even convince her to enter a family pact with him. There are plenty of skilled programmers to take his place on Hissa. His people won't suffer due to his absence. And many others, eager to prove themselves, will be thrilled to partake in another mission attempt to Bicoma. He needn't feel guilt over that.

He does briefly wonder about the fate of his crew mates again and that makes him murmur out the ancient Hissa prayer to Brimming and Diminish, the two moons of Hissa.

"What about this one?" Mara asks him, drawing his attention to the large display she's pointing to. He realizes she's been talking to him, but he was too lost in thought to hear her. Again. If he keeps this up, she'll think he's become addle-brained. Snorting at that thought, he studies the display. It's covered in rows and rows of shipping timetables and routes.

"I can afford to get you on that one." She points to a slow-moving, old, metal trawler ship. The contract notes the trawler's willing to take on three passengers and no spaces are filled yet.

"I know this ship. The captain and crew can be trusted." She points to another passenger contract up for sale. "This one is the same price on a faster ship, but I don't know them. They might be legitimate, or they might just be waiting for victims to sign up for passage."

"Victims?"

"There are several mining colonies close by that don't ask many questions about where their slave labor comes from. Sometimes, to earn some easy credits, ships will sell passengers to the colonies. It's easy to end up a slave in this sector and almost impossible to get free again."

"I didn't know this was such an issue," he admits, feeling strangely naïve. Becoming a slave isn't something Hissa normally need to worry about. The more time he spends with Mara, the more he realizes what a dangerous universe it is to be human and alone.

"Don't worry. I'm going to make damn sure that doesn't happen to you again. That's why the trawler is your best option. I know the captain, and I can afford it."

"Afford?" He's not sure what she's talking about.

Chuckling, she gives him an affectionate hug. "Yeah. Afford. Most haulers aren't sweet like me. They aren't going to haul you around for free, no matter how handsome you are. But with what I just got paid, I can get you a seat on this one. I don't want you to have to work for passage. That can get sticky fast if they decide to be difficult."

"I don't want you to pay for me."

Rubbing his back soothingly, she gives him a reassuring smile. "I want to pay. I want to help you. If you don't want to go back to Hissa, I can give you some credits to set yourself up here as a programmer. I know for a fact they need one here. The bio-system algorithms are always messing up one end of the station or the other."

This isn't going at all like he planned. If she wasn't so altruistic it would be easier to convince her to let him work for her simply for food and shelter. If she'd stop being so damn noble and trying to send him home, this would all be much easier.

"You've already given me too much. Why are you being

so generous to me?"

Face softening, she stills her hand on his back. "It was a shit deal that you got kidnapped and sold."

"You were sold," Tiran points out. "No one rescued you."

"That's different. I never knew what freedom was. I think it's different if you never know what it's like to be free before you become a slave. Back then, I didn't know what freedom was. But now, I could never go back to being a slave. If all you know is slavery, it's easier to deal with. If you've been free, then become a slave, that life breaks you."

Her honesty touches him, and he wants to hold her. He grabs her up in a bear hug, hauling her off the ground. Burying his face in her neck, he inhales her wonderful scent. "I promise no one will ever take away your freedom again."

Bringing her arms up, she hugs him back just as fiercely. "I'm fine, big guy" she whispers in a husky voice. "I get to say no now. And I can fight. No one will ever buy me or hurt me again."

"That's why you refused Tifle's offer of four hundred credits. That number of credits would be enough to buy almost an entire dimmerion control panel, but you didn't even hesitate to tell him no."

"No money will ever be enough to buy me again," she tells him. "Even for a few hours. Even if there is a release clause that protects me from physical damage. Freedom is too precious to give up for something like credits."

He couldn't agree with her more and opens his mouth to tell her just that when the hall where they're standing is suddenly crowded. He tries to move the two of them aside to let the newcomers access the shipping board information, but they don't move any closer to the board.

"We need you to come with us," a voice states, and Tiran looks over to find the two guards from earlier along with four more of equal or greater size. Each one has a shock stick, and one of them is holding an obedience collar. "The female needs to come with us. It's only for a few days; then she'll be released. Don't make us hurt either of you."

"Crap," Mara curses under her breath. "No cameras down here."

Turning, he gently sets Mara against the wall where the shipping schedule displays are secured. "Stay," he orders her, giving her a big grin that shows off his massive canines. "I go to prove my worth now."

Then he turns back to the guards and roars before launching himself at the closest one.

CHAPTER

14

Mara can only stand there and gape as Tiran barrels into the guard holding the collar. The large alien is knocked back into two others. All three find themselves scrambling for balance. While they're distracted, Tiran turns on the next closest guard who's about to hit him on the head with his shock stick. The guy's trying to use it as a blunt weapon instead of its intended purpose. Poorly trained idiot!

Tiran easily avoids the blow and brings a punch to the guard's face. The blow only dazes the guard. He snarls and tries to bring the shock stick down again, but he doesn't have a chance to even bring his arm up before Tiran hits him with a blow to the sternum. The guard gasps and falls to his knees, the shock stick rolling until it stops against Mara's foot.

Grabbing it, she makes sure it's active and brings it up, ready to join the fight only to find Tiran has paused long enough to catch her eye.

"Don't interfere." He's holding one guard in the air by the throat.

Although she's scared for both of them, she raises an eyebrow and pretends nonchalance. Crossing her arms and leaning against the wall, she nods to the guard choking in his grip and smirks.

"Have fun, handsome."

And it seems like he does.

It becomes obvious quickly that the guards are used to using their superior size to win physical altercations. Most of them throw clumsy punches with little skill. Their footwork is poor at best, and they don't know how to defend against a blow very well. But they're also big, tough, and not easily knocked out.

When Tiran goes flying and hits the wall next to her, she tries to kneel next to him to assess the damage, but he's up before she can even touch him.

"Stay!" he commands and throws himself back into the fray.

Shaking her head at the amount of abuse the big Hissa can take, she watches him fight multiple opponents. She could handle one of these guards if she were by herself, perhaps even two. Six guards would've meant her capture and enslavement. But Tiran is working his way through them as if he feels no pain. His skill, stamina, and sheer brute strength are as terrifying as impressive. He's not quite as fast as she is, but he makes up for that with raw power, intensity, and endurance.

One of the guards goes flying and Mara has to jump to the side to avoid him. He hits the ground, and she steps up and shocks him a few times until he's still. Tiran sees her do it and frowns at her at the same time he's pounding his fist repeatedly into another guard's face.

"Hey, a girl's gotta have some fun," she calls out. A toothy grin takes the place of his frown. It makes her melt a little inside even as thick, gooey, green blood shoots out of the guard's nose, splashing on Tiran's chest.

Three of the guards are down now, but Tiran is starting to move slower. Mara can see several of the guards have landed blows on his face and torso. He's not using his right hand any longer to punch and the way one finger is sticking out oddly tells Mara a bone or two may be broken.

It's lucky for both of them that the guards aren't used to fighting as a unit. They're clumsy with each other, often getting in each other's way instead of helping. Mara manages to kick a foot out and shoves one guard into another. In a move worthy of an old Earth comedy the two hit heads so hard they're both dazed.

Tiran's too busy dealing with the last remaining guard to notice when Mara shocks them both to unconsciousness.

Wincing when the last guard delivers a stunning blow to Tiran's head, she watches with concern as the big man ends up on one knee. When Mara moves to intercede, the guard's gaze locks on her and he starts to step toward her, ready to claim the prize. Tucking the spent shock stick in her belt, she brings her fists up, flashing the guy a defiant grin.

"Bring it! I've taken down bigger than you!"

The guard's almost to her when his face goes slack, and he falls at her feet. She looks up to see Tiran standing there holding a shock stick of his own. He meets her eyes and smiles ruefully. "I don't consider that cheating." He holds up the shock stick. "They used one on me earlier. It's only fair I get to use it too."

Astonished Tiran's still standing, she nods her head and looks around at the six unconscious guards. "How did you do that?" Sure, she'd shocked a few of them, but they'd already been on the ground at the time.

"It took a great deal of effort," Tiran admits and sways a little on his feet. Mara rushes up to him and draws one of his big arms around her shoulders, curling her arm around his torso. He winces at the pressure but doesn't complain as he leans into her. "I'd like to fall down now. Could you take me someplace soft?"

"No collapsing yet," she promises. "The bunk on Witch is as soft as I can offer."

"Perfect," he grunts; then he closes his eyes and lets her guide him back. It seems to take forever to get him to Witch, and she just manages to get him to the bunk before his legs give out entirely.

"Witch, get us out of here. Situation is urgent. Minimum safe distance is to be calculated as whatever is outside of station hailing range."

The ship rumbles to life as she un-docks, making Mara sigh with relief as they move away from Gleem. This was only her second time there, and she promises herself it will be her last.

She wonders if it's her or the station, but her last visit ended with a fight also. Last time it was just a quick brawl that was broken up by station security almost the moment it got started. This time, however, it could've been so much worse. If Tiran wasn't with her, she'd be in a collar again.

She knows he wants to stay with her. He might think she's clueless or ignorant to all his hints and offers, but she knows he doesn't want to leave Witch to go back to Hissa or find an alternate job on a station. She resisted letting him stay. She likes her solitary life. And she needs to be able to focus on finding her sister.

And yet, this big Hissa just saved her from captivity. He put himself in mortal danger to keep her from being a slave again. That kind of loyalty is invaluable. Besides, a strange kind of pain started filling her chest as she talked to him about buying passage. The two of them parting ways doesn't feel right.

Since they're both back on board the ship, together until at least the next station, she decides there's no need for any kind of soul searching. There will be enough time enough to think about their future later. For right now, Tiran needs some looking after considering the pounding he received.

She examines him with a critical eye. His green skin is paler than she likes. He might not be getting enough air and that worries her much more than the hand injury.

"I want to take a look at your chest with the scanner," she tells him as she starts undoing his biosuit. Better to check for internal injuries now while she's close to a station with a medical unit. For Tiran, she'd brave Gleem again if he needs more than what her paltry med kit can provide.

"You don't need to scan me," Tiran says without

opening his eyes. "I know I'm not too badly damaged. But if you feel the need to have me naked so you can use my body for your pleasure that would be fine."

Snorting out a laugh, she puts a gentle hand on his shoulder, needing to touch him. "That was a hell of a fight. I don't think I've seen it's equal," she admits. "Let me just do a quick scan to check."

"I'd know if anything was broken. I'm only bruised." He holds up his right hand. "Except for this. I believe there might be a break in this hand. Let me see."

She watches him grasp his right hand in his left hand, frowning as he feels for a break. "Ah, no, it's just dislocated," he says at the same time he jerks his right thumb with his left hand, and Mara hears a popping sound. Tiran gives a relieved sigh and drops his arms onto his chest. "That's better."

"I can't believe you just did that," she states with a shudder. The sound of his joint popping into place is going to haunt her for a while.

Turning his head toward her, he watches her with half-lidded eyes. "Didn't you want to get my clothes off?"

"I guess you can't be too hurt if that's on your mind," she snickers, pleased he can make jokes. Her scowling, growling Hissa has suddenly been replaced by a battered but happy warrior.

Rolling into a more comfortable position he closes his eyes. "Are we under way?"

"The moment we got inside the hatch," she confirms. "I didn't think it was prudent to stick around. I'd rather not give Tifle another chance to earn his four hundred credits."

"But where are we going?" he asks absently, his words slurring together at the end. She thinks he's falling asleep but then his body jolts. Opening his eyes, he grabs one of her hands and brings it to his chest, drawing her closer to him. "You're not taking me to another place to drop me off, are you?"

"Easy there. I'm not taking you anywhere right now," Mara assures him. "Witch doesn't have a destination. I just wanted to get us away from the station. Once she's far enough away, she'll just hang until I tell her where to go."

"You didn't have time to find a contract to haul cargo," Tiran states anxiously. "I need to get you credits. You need fuel and supplies."

"Don't worry. I've got enough credits to refuel at Santin Port. That's not far. Then we can figure out how to get you home," she promises him.

He relaxes at her words, he doesn't let go of her hand. "You take me," he demands as if he expects obedience because it's the only logical outcome. It reminds her a little of when he demanded to be released from the bunk after she shared her story with him.

"I can't take you all the way to Hissa," she explains to him with real regret. Nothing would please her more than becoming a passenger hauler for just Tiran. "But there's no way I could afford all the fuel to get you there without another paying job."

Lids starting to droop again, he waves his free hand in the air as if brushing away her concerns. "I'll pay you. Anything you need, I can pay for."

"I must have missed all the credits you were carrying around," she says dryly. "Where did you hide them when you were naked and being sold as a slave?"

Sighing at her, he shakes his head and looks resigned. "I don't have anything with me. But back on Hissa I have enough wealth to buy you another Witch if you like."

"Sure you do, handsome. You just rest for now. I'll take care of you. You can impress me with all your credits some other time."

He tries to draw her down to join him in the bed, but she resists, and he stops tugging at her. "Bad idea. I'll just get comfy next to the bed for now. I don't want to hurt you by accident."

With a faint smile he resumes tugging on her. "Your distance is hurting me more."

Letting him pull her down, she makes sure to snuggle against him instead of on top of him. It's a squeeze, but she manages to fit herself into the bunk and keep from doing any further damage to his already battered body.

It's comforting to be next to his big, warm body and feel his chest rising and falling under her hand. "You know, you're magnificent when you fight."

"Thank you." He nuzzles her hair and tries to slide her hand south.

"Stop that," she admonishes and pushes her hand back up on his chest. "You're not fit for any kind of exercise. Close your eyes and rest for a bit."

"You could do all the work."

"Rest, or I'll leave the bed," she threatens, and he stops trying to move her hand. Within moments he starts snoring.

CHAPTER

15

Tiran wakes to find Mara hunched over the control console's display, muttering to herself and frowning. He's surprised he didn't wake up when she left the bunk, but then again, his body had a lot of damage to heal. He remains quiet and still on the bunk so he can take a moment to observe her without her being aware of it. Her long black hair is loose, hanging over her shoulders to pool on the console in front of her. Every line of her sleek, muscled body is visible through the tight biosuit. He might be strength and power, but she's speed and grace.

Even with irritation showing on her face, she's beautiful.

Thanks be to the moons that the little Fozin tried to sell Mara. Not that he's glad some faceless buyer is enamored of her, but that the panicked Fozin sent six large males to try and capture her. He couldn't have hoped for a better way to prove himself. Six had been a bit much, but still, it allowed him to show Mara his worth as a warrior and protector.

Of course, her first impression of him couldn't get much worse considering she first laid eyes on him while he stood naked, in a collar, waiting to be auctioned. The fact that he was naked doesn't bother him because he knows his body drew her attention as much as his roars.

He didn't tell her, but one of those roars was specifically to get her to look at him so he could see her eyes. The hit with the shock stick was worth it. He knows he'd be a terrible slave. If anyone but Mara had bought him, he'd probably be dead, or wishing he were dead, within a few days. But Mara had bought him, and that makes the whole thing worth it.

What would it be like to be born a slave? His chest constricts at the thought of little Mara, tiny and vulnerable, created with the intention of never knowing freedom. When she shared her story, she casually mentioned getting a job in space, but she couldn't have done it so easily. She probably worked for room and board at first, doing the worst and most dangerous jobs. Working her way up in the crew over years. She would've needed to be so many things to survive; tough, smart, resilient, tenacious, and courageous. He's not sure he would've had the fortitude to survive her life. He doesn't think many could.

Clever and strong Mara, saving her credits to buy sickly Witch. Kind and caring Mara who nursed the ship back to health. Gracious Mara, who used almost all her credits to buy him. Fierce Mara, who kicked his ass when he tried to capture her.

The memory makes him grin.

Gorgeous Mara who smells so delectable. Who screams so beautifully when feeling intense pleasure.

And that memory makes him hard.

He's sure the fight on Gleem put him in a better place to ask Mara to enter a family pact with him. Even if they can't have children, they could search out other Decanted slaves and save them. They could buy them and then set them free but not leave them without resources. Each one could be adopted into their Family Pact, thereby making sure they have a safe home on Hissa.

The next step in his plan is getting them both to Hissa. He needs to make arrangements with his people so he can stay with her. And he desperately wants to show her his wealth. He has a few contacts in the military. They might be able to help search for her sister. And of course, he can prove to her he's capable of financially supporting her and Witch. She'll never need to worry about food, fuel, or anything else again. He could care for her and keep her safe. No more dangerous space docks. No more scrounging for contracts. No more fear of raider attacks or kidnapping by slavers. They'll search for her sister together. Rescue Decanted humans together.

He could take all her fears away. All he needs to do is get her to Hissa.

She mutters again darkly and stabs her finger at the display a few times. Tiran isn't concerned. He's seen her interact with the control console enough to know this isn't out of character for her. He watches with amusement as she curses in several different languages and pokes viciously at the display. A small tentacle emerges from high on the console deck and swats playfully at Mara's hand, drawing her out of her dark mutterings and making her laugh. She plays with Witch for a few moments, then goes back to staring at the display.

Finally, she sits back with a satisfied expression and pats the display instead of poking at it. Curious, Tiran sits up and stretches his arms, making her aware that he's awake.

She looks over and grins at him. "I think I've got it worked out." He tilts his head inquiringly, and she nods enthusiastically. "If we sling-shot around a couple of planets, we have just enough fuel to get to Hissa. I doubt you're as rich as you claim, but you'd better be able to at least fuel me up or I'm going to be stuck there."

"Would that be so horrible?" he asks. "My home world is a nice place. Pretty and modern. There are worst planets to spend time on."

"Oh, and I did a little check earlier while I still had com links to Gleem. There's no such thing as being Dishonored on Hissa or anything like that," she accuses him as she stands up to face him. She crosses her arms over her chest and taps a foot on the floor. Instead of a guilty confession or at least a look of contrition, he stands tall and gives her a big unrepentant grin.

"You're very compassionate," he states, and he can see Mara resisting the urge to throw something at him. "After you told me your story, I believed you. I had no intention of attacking you again, but you didn't want to release the restraints. So, I needed to make you feel sympathy for me. You have a generous heart."

"Did you just compliment me for falling for a line of Pienter shit?" Mara asks with mild scorn.

"No," Tiran tells her, the grin not diminishing. "I'm complimenting you for being kind despite your hard life. You could've left me unconscious at the station after I tried to subdue you. Dumped on the dock, at the mercy of whoever came across my helpless body. But you didn't. You kept me and cared for me and went to great pains to make me feel safe and secure."

It's obvious by her expression that his words are knocking her off the mountain of mad she originally climbed up on. She must have expected denial from him or a fight. Anything but compliments.

"I…" Mara starts but can't seem to finish her sentence. Her expression looks both irritated and pleased, as if she's not sure which direction her emotions should take.

"And then you examined me and touched me, and that was even better," he finishes with a lascivious grin.

That makes her roll her eyes and huff out an annoyed sound, but he can tell she's fighting not to smile. "Males are the same in just about every species." She walks over to join him on the bunk. "So, we've got about five days until we get to Hissa."

"Five days. There are a lot of repairs we could attempt to get done in that time."

Leaning in close, she brushes her lips against his cheek. "That's true. The bio-system recyclers need to be cleaned."

Catching her jaw with his hand, he gives her a chaste kiss on the lips. "I could do a little more programming. The thruster controls need more fine tuning." He turns his head to bury his nose against her neck. She makes a happy sound when he grazes his teeth along her skin.

Moving her hand into his lap, she finds his already swelling cock. He gives a little groan when she squeezes. He adores her strong hands. He nips her neck with his teeth with a little more force, making her shudder.

"And I should stow all the tools and stuff in the cargo hold." She sounds a little breathless as she talks. With a sigh, she slides off the bunk and puts herself between his knees. "We just left it all lying around after the repairs."

"It's a danger to have tools lose and unattended," he agrees and promptly starts pulling at all the closures to his biosuit.

"Let's get right on that," she murmurs as he stands up to help slide the suit off his body. Cool air hits his overheated skin. She drops back down to her knees just as he turns slightly, almost smacking her in the face with his erection.

Giggling, she grabs his bobbing erection and gives it a little squeeze. Tiran hisses and freezes. "I want to taste you," she tells him. He makes a sound of protest, worrying his size might hurt her, and tries to pull away. She hastily draws the tip of him into her mouth and he stops resisting. Groaning, he reaches to grasp the storage locker over the bunk to steady himself. He's never felt anything like this before.

"I haven't ever..." he starts to say, but Mara draws him further into her mouth, and he groans and finds he can't talk.

He watches her take as much of him into her mouth as she can, struck speechless by the wet heat of her. Even though he can tell she's not breathing very well with his length pushing against the back of her throat, she won't let him pull away. Before he starts to panic, she pulls back a little, taking air in through her nose. She reaches up with both hands, holding the base of his shaft with one and cupping his balls with the other.

It's amazing that his body can remain standing when there's no blood in his head.

"Please," he croaks out and watches the corners of her lips curve in aroused amusement at his plea. He wants to beg for more. Wants her to swallow him down again and draw him out. Wants her fingers to quicken their too slow rhythm. He wants all these things, but he can't seem to put them into words. All he can say is, "My beautiful Mara." And then let her do with him whatever she wishes.

Moving forward, she slides him back into her mouth, covering the part she can't fit inside her mouth with her hand, using her saliva to rub and stroke the base. With her other hand, she gently tugs at his scrotum. The sensations are so intense that he's sure it might be considered torture in some cultures.

His body is shaking now, with tremors moving down his legs. He's close, and he wants to tell her to stop and pull away from him. He can't imagine she wants to keep him in her mouth while he climaxes, and he worries he'll offend her. He opens his mouth to talk, to warn her. He tells his hands to let go of the storage locker he's holding with a death grip. But his body can't seem to obey either order, and with a helpless moan he comes in her mouth.

Body stiffening, he tries to jerk away from her, but she must have been prepared for this because she wraps her arms around the back of his legs and sucks even harder on his throbbing cock as if he's a treat she craves. She doesn't stop until there's nothing left inside of him and he's making helpless noises deep in his chest.

When she finally releases him and sits back on her heels, Tiran lets go of the cabinet and thumps down on the bunk looking dazed.

"I...I...," he starts, but has to clear his throat a few times before he can continue. "It's never been like that. No one has ever..." he takes a deep breath of air and leans forward to wrap his arms around her. He sits up, dragging her onto his lap, and just hugs her. She wraps her legs around his waist and hugs him back, making a little sound of happiness.

"Thank you," he whispers into her ear.

"It wasn't a hardship," she whispers back. "You taste good. A girl could get addicted." That makes him choke a little.

"Then we have that in common," he tells her, laughing now. Holding her against his chest, he stands up with Mara still clinging to him. He pulls her off him and sets her on her feet, then grabs two fistfuls of her biosuit. She makes a warning sound and grabs his wrists to stop him.

"Hold on, big guy," she tells him. "Don't tear this one. These things are expensive!"

Tiran doesn't feel like joking anymore. He can buy her hundreds of the blasted biosuits, but he can't buy more time with her, so he needs her naked and against him now. "Get it off," he growls. Taken a little aback, she stiffens and doesn't reach for the suit closures. "Get it off or I'll tear it off whether you like it or not."

"Easy there," she warns him, giving him a look that's both annoyed and wary. "Don't turn this into something ugly."

Closing his eyes, he takes a few deep breaths, realizing he's letting his primitive side get the better of him. "I'm sorry. I feel very savage at the moment. I need to feel your skin. I need to taste you." He pauses and opens his eyes. "I feel like I need this as much as I need my next breath of air. I can't describe it, but suddenly I feel this pressure in me." He taps his chest with his open palm as he tries to describe what's going on. "It's intense and painful. Please hurry to take off suit. I'll stand here and be patient. I have control."

Nodding her head, she accepts his words at face value and starts pulling the closures open. Suit, panties, and bra end up in a small heap next to her feet. No sooner is she naked than he grabs her and lays her out on the bed with a speed that takes her breath away.

"You smell like yourself and me," he tells her as he lays down on top of her. "It's driving me crazy."

Before she can respond he puts his mouth on her. He sucks and nibbles at her until she moans, then gives her a little nip. Her feminine smell fills his nose.

"You're wet for me," he breathes and moves his body down hers until his head is between her legs. "I've barely done anything, and you're already ready for me." She whimpers a little when he roughly shoves her thighs apart and takes a deep breath. "You smell better than anything. Your scent does things to me." Then his lips are on her. Parting her wet labia, he gives into the need to fill his mouth with her and sinks his tongue into her warmth. She moves a little under him and he grabs her hips to hold her still so his mouth can work. She stills when his big hands grip her, only pulsing under him a little as her body reacts to the pleasure.

She makes a needy mewling sound as he laps at her, but when he finds her clit with his mouth, she can't stay remotely still. She bucks hard against his hold, sobbing with need. He uses his superior strength to hold her down, noticing she seems to want to strain against him. She's not fighting to get away. The stronger he holds her the more she seems to like it and soon she's thrashing her hips and legs in his hold.

Then she's screaming as she comes, grabbing and tearing at the bedding around her, even scratching at his shoulders. He can feel her nails digging into his flesh, but it doesn't hurt. When he finally draws away from her, she's gasping while shudders ricochet through her body.

Moving to lie next to her, he pulls her limp body to him in a tight embrace and sighs with contentment. The scent of sex is heavy in the air, and they are both covered in sweat. He hears her mumble something about cleaning up and he just holds her tightly in his arms.

"Nap now," he orders with a nuzzle. She can only nod. She's not ready to form words yet. "Rest now. Everything else later." He feels her body slacken into slumber just before sleep overtakes him as well.

CHAPTER

16

A soft chime sound wakes them both from their sleep. Mara groans but Tiran rises, eager to start the day. "Up," he tells her. "We'll be at Hissa soon."

Opening one bleary eye, she gives him a malevolent look, but the effect is ruined by her tangled mess of hair falling in her face. She pushes it out of the way to more effectively glare at him. "Stop being so damn cheerful," she orders. "No one should wake up so cheerful. Waking up is painful. You should look pained."

He gives her a playful slap on her naked ass. "I'm excited to show you my home." Keeping his hand on her naked backside, he lowers his face and gives her a quick nip.

Glowering at him, she shoves him away from her. "Just get off me, you big oaf. I'm going to shower. And eat. Only then will I possibly be able to put up with your exuberance."

Instead of looking appropriately contrite, he laughs and obediently gets off her and strides naked to the control console to look at their location and fuel status. Admiring the view as he moves, she licks her lips, wondering if they have time for one more quick romp before they go planet-side.

Maybe she should try and seduce him back into bed. They could orbit the planet for a few more days, letting the two of them hole up on Witch for a bit longer before facing whatever is waiting for him planet-side. She's about to open her mouth to invite him back to the bunk and her warm body when he gives a little shout of joy.

"I've received a message from Father! The other men, crewmates, men on my ship, they are recovered. One is inbound. Another is carrying on mission. Excellent news this." It's cute when his accent goes thick, and his language skills deteriorate from excitement instead of anger or concern.

He'd confessed to her his deep concern for his missing crewmates and the mission they'd failed to fulfill. It's good to know everyone's alive, and there's still hope for Hissa to receive help from Bicoma.

"That's great news."

He nods but doesn't look up from the screen. "My father's overjoyed I'm returned safely. Wants to meet you very much." He's so excited he's almost wiggling like a puppy, but Mara feels a little pinch of dread tighten her stomach. She's not Hissa. She's not even really fully human. She's a Decanted and a former slave. What will Tiran's father think of her when he finds out they're lovers?

The cabin suddenly seems too warm. And too small, and the air feels thick.

"I'm going to grab a quick shower," she tells him and grabs her clothes and dashes to the bathroom before he can respond. Outside of the cargo hold is the only other place on Witch where she can close a door and be alone.

In the small room, she calls for the shower stall and water on. Witch knows what temperature she likes, and hot water starts flowing over her. She feels safe enough in the bathroom to let a few tears trickle down her face.

In just a few hours she might have to say goodbye to her big Hissa warrior. The thought makes her heart hurt. She wants to sob. But most of all she wants to wrap her arms around him and not let him go.

"I'll come back," she promises herself and scrubs away the useless tears. "I'll find my sister and come back."

But how long would that take? Years? Would Tiran even remember her by the time she could make it back to him? The only people she's ever felt as close to as Tiran were Captain Dolan and her sister. What if he finds another female he likes better? Another human that isn't Decanted. Another human that was never owned as property.

The thought feels like a stab to her heart.

The idea of him finding another female hurts but it's not fair to ask Tiran to wait for her. Or to come with her. He has responsibilities to his people. He can't just go off with her on an endless and potentially fruitless search for Lara.

If the one Hissa crewmate is completing the mission, what will he find out from the Bicoma? Maybe they'll know about a species that's breeding compatible. Then the Hissa could start negotiations for females from that species. What if Tiran takes a wife while she's away?

What did he call the Hissa version of marriage? Family Pact. What if he signed a Family Pact with another female?

The image of some faceless female touching Tiran makes her go hot with anger. "Fuck this," she mutters to herself and barely keeps from punching the shower wall.

"Cold water," Mara calls out and relishes the shock to her system when the cold water flows over her, chilling her skin and calming her anger. She's about to call out to Witch to turn off the water when the door opens, and Tiran joins her in the shower.

He yelps at the cold temperature and Mara quickly calls out, "Warm water."

"That was freezing," he says, regarding her with concern. "Why would you want the water so cold?" He reaches out and draws her into his arms. "Your body is cold. What were you thinking?"

"It's fine," she tells him, forcing herself to smile. "It's

just something I do sometimes to wake up."

Shaking his head, he rubs his hands up and down her arms. "I'll wake you up. I'm much better than cold water." That makes Mara's smile real. She moves to hug him; except he makes an odd noise and pushes her away. Holding her at arm's length, he stares at her neck, eyes full of shock and disbelief.

"What?" She looks down at herself, trying to figure out what's wrong. All her bruises are gone. There isn't a mark or dark spot anywhere on her.

"Your neck and shoulders," he chokes out.

Mara looks down and sees a faint red color on one shoulder. Maybe she gave herself a little bit of a burn with the hot water. Witch might be having issues with some of her controls because of Tiran's poking about in the control console. Because of her odd biology sometimes she doesn't register pain sensations like a normal human would. It's rare, but it's happened to her before.

"Witch, mirror, full length," Mara calls out, and one side of the shower stall turns into a large reflective surface. Turning away from Tiran, she looks at herself in the mirror and gasps.

The base of her neck and top of her shoulders don't look burned; they look tattooed in a tight, red, swirling pattern. As it nears the ends of her shoulders, the pattern becomes less and less distinct, until it's just the light red coloring she mistook for a burn.

"What's going on?" she whispers and leans closer to the mirror to touch the marking. She can't feel anything under her fingers. No raised skin, no pain.

Wordlessly, she turns to Tiran. "Do you think this is some weird rash? I've never been sick, never gotten anything. Maybe this is something to do with my odd genetics?" A thought hits her, making her pale and sway a little. "What if I'm susceptible to Hissa diseases?"

Expression unreadable, Tiran shakes his head. "I don't have any disease," he tells her bluntly, staring intently at the markings on her neck and shoulders. She wants to hug him, but he looks almost angry at her.

"But you could be a carrier," she tells him. "Oh shit, do I have your plague?"

It never occurred to her that she could die from a disease, and she finds the prospect terrifying. Tiran's expression softens a little, and he draws her into his arms. "It's not the plague. I promise."

Laying her cheek on his chest, she lets his confidence comfort her. "I wouldn't blame you," she assures him. "If I died from a plague, I wouldn't be mad at you. I'd just be sad that I couldn't find my sister."

"It's not the plague," he repeats, his arms tightening around her. He kisses the top of her head. "You're healthy. Let's go down to Hissa. I want to show you my homeworld, and I think we might find an answer down there."

Strange markings forgotten, she nods her head and calls for Witch to shut off the water. Time to face Tiran's people. "Sure, we can visit. Just make sure you take good care of Witch if I up and die on you because I caught your disease." Her tone falls a little short of the teasing quality she was going for.

Patting her back soothingly, he makes a soft comforting noise. "I promise you won't die. Trust me."

"I do," she tells him.

And that's what love is, she thinks. Trust. At least that's what love is for her.

By the time the shuttle sent from the planet's surface docks with Witch, Mara starts to wish, just a little, that she had a serious illness. Then she could have an excuse to stay on Witch.

She doesn't visit planet-side very often. Almost her entire freedom has been spent in space; on ships, space ports, and stations. She can count on one hand the number of times she's stepped on terra firma after escaping captivity. To her, planets are where people like her are trapped, forced into servitude, and abused on a whim. Planets are not safe places.

She wants to tell Tiran all this, but he looks so eager when the shuttle docks that the words die in her throat. Bracing herself to meet new Hissa when the hatch opens, she's surprised to find the shuttle empty. Tiran hurries forward and picks up a small box that's been stowed on one of the seats. Impatiently, he opens it as he walks back to her.

"I asked them to remote pilot the shuttle to us," he explains. "I didn't want anyone fresh from the planet potentially carrying anything up to us before I could make you safe. I didn't want to risk you getting the plague." He holds up a drug gun and moves toward her. Throwing up her hands, she backs away warily.

"Whoa, hold off there. What's in that?"

Although he stops, he casts her a look of pure irritation. "The vaccine to the plague that killed so many of us. I sent the body Menders and scientists information on you, and they made this especially for your biology."

Blood drains from her face, fear swamping her system. Tiran grabs her before she can fall, tucking the drug gun under his arm. She looks up to him, anxiety filling her chest. "I thought you said I didn't have the plague."

The sound of her trembling voice fills her with disgust. What's wrong with her? Normally she's ready to face down danger, but for some reason the twin fears of going planet-side and potentially catching a deadly, painful disease are swamping her ability to cope.

"You don't! I know what the symptoms are. You don't have them. This is a vaccine, so you don't get the plague. There isn't a cure if you do get it," he explains. "Please let me give this to you. I don't know if you're susceptible to our disease, but it would make me feel better to know you're protected."

Taking a deep breath, she wills her heartbeat to slow. She's never been this fearful, not since waking up in the rescue ship without her sister all those years ago. She's stronger than this. She refuses to be a panicky mess.

Stiffening her spine and squaring her shoulders, she unfastens the very top of her biosuit to expose her lower neck and shoulder. "Do it."

Giving her a relieved smile, he presses the drug gun to her neck. She feels a slight pressure, then it's over. Tiran tosses the drug gun and gathers her up into a tight hug.

"Thank you, Mara," he murmurs in a low voice. She feels herself shiver a little at that voice and wraps her arms around his waist and moves her body against his.

"How long does it take to get to the planet's surface?" she asks suggestively while kissing his neck.

"Not long enough," he chuckles. He picks her up, ignoring her little squeal of protest, and sets her down on a seat inside the shuttle. Even though she can do it herself, she lets him secure her in the seat. The care he takes to adjust the straps to her smaller height makes her heart want to burst with love. It's a small, simple thing, but it means so much to her. He means so much to her.

"Sit there and behave," he admonishes as he makes himself comfortable at the shuttle controls.

Witch shuts the hatch and releases the shuttle. Once released, Tiran takes over the control of the shuttle from the remote pilot on the ground and flies the small craft to the planet's surface. His flying isn't the most skilled she's experienced. Actually, he's a horrible pilot, and if the shuttle wasn't so advanced as to compensate for his poor skills, she's sure they'd crash. In an attempt to take her mind off Tiran's lack of technique, she examines the planet below.

The planet's surface details coalesce as they get closer and closer to the landing pad. Tiran didn't exaggerate. His planet is beautiful. For as far as she can see, there is nothing but green, lush land outside the city. Automated trams run in a spoke wheel formation from village to village, all feeding into the large central urban area. Just about all the houses and city buildings are round, many with domed roofs. She wonders if that's for aesthetics or practical purposes.

From what she can see, the houses located outside the denser city center are quaint, surrounded by dense, lush foliage full of bright flowers with small paths leading from house to house. Each home has a large, well-tended, colorful garden.

As the Hissa city gets closer, she's shocked at how clean and orderly everything is. Stone seems to be the favorite building material. They've used a combination of roughhewn stone, interspersed with elaborately carved edifices. Even the streets are decorated with designs and motifs. She wants to ask what the designs mean, but Tiran is focused, and she doesn't want to bother him. Relaxing, she takes everything in.

No litter. No vagrants. No seedy streets filled with illegal markets and questionable characters. Most of the buildings have vegetation growing on one or two sides, and she wonders how they keep the other sides free of plants. Keeping the jungle from swallowing the villages and cities must require a great deal of effort.

She remembers Tiran telling her the Hissa are a rich people because both their moons are full of rare minerals. Most Hissa work directly or indirectly for either their mining industry or the military. Their wealth means they've been attacked many times in the past by other species eager to steal Hissa wealth.

The money that flows from the mining also means there's a myriad of goods they can afford to import. He admitted, almost sheepishly, that the Hissa don't manufacture much anymore, preferring to import what they need. He did tell her with satisfaction about Hissa food production and their excellent farms and gardens. That's a point of pride with every Hissa.

As they land, Mara notices a small group of Hissa men standing there, waiting for them. It's easy for her to pick out Tiran's father. The resemblance is unmistakable. He looks to be a little taller than Tiran, with the same broad, muscular build and commanding presence. The men around him aren't tiny either. All the Hissa men gathered are huge and gauging by the small sample size of men waiting for them, Tiran and his father are on the smaller side.

"You said your name meant tree," she calls to him as they touch the ground. He laughs.

"They named me Tree because I was small when I was born. It was a joke that stuck because my mother decided that naming me Tree would make me strong. Tall trees can break in the wind; shorter, stocky trees can resist and remain."

That makes Mara smile. "She was a smart woman."

"She was wonderful. So is my father. You'll like him."

Mara feels the shuttle touch down, and the engines immediately cut off. Before she can move, Tiran is there, unbuckling her from the seat and lifting her out. He doesn't set her down but cuddles her to his chest like a child. She smacks him on the shoulder.

"Stop it! I'm done being all scared or nervous. I'm good. Just let me walk."

Tiran hesitates, then sets her on her feet. "You'll tell me if you don't feel well? I know you're a little anxious about my planet and people. Please don't be. They'll all adore you."

"I'll be fine," she promises and hopes he's right. She's not sure how she'll handle it if his father hates her and sends her packing right away. She's hoping for at least one more night with Tiran.

The hatch opens and warm, moist air fills the cabin along with the smell of fresh air, vegetation, blossoming flowers, and sweet ripe fruit.

Taking her hand, he gives it a gentle tug until she follows him out. The men don't seem surprised to see her, so Tiran or his father must have told them about her. Tiran's father strides forward. He stops a stride away and taps his two fingers between his eyes. After Tiran makes the gesture back, he grabs Tiran in a bear-hug, lifting his son into the air and setting him back down with a grunt. Tiran makes an irritated noise, but it's obvious he's pleased with his father's actions.

"I'm a grown male," he chides his father, pushing the older man off. To her relief, Tiran is speaking in Space Standard, and his father responds in the same language.

"You'll always be my son," his father counters. His Space Standard is so perfect he doesn't even have an accent.

"It's good to have you home," he tells Tiran. "I was so very worried when we didn't hear an update from you. We all feared the worst."

"I'm safe, thanks to Mara," Tiran announces loud enough for the rest of the men to hear. "She saved me by buying me at a slave auction but tortured me by refusing to make me her sex slave." The men all laugh appreciatively, and Mara feels a flush spread across her face. She wants to smack him, but before she can admonish him for such a crude joke, his father is in front of her. He taps his two fingers against his chest, then gathers her in a gentle hug and lifts her in the air very much like he did with Tiran.

"Thank you, dear woman," he says. "My name is Nelam. You saved my son and my only family. Anything I have is yours for the asking."

She's about to tell him it wasn't a big deal and all she needs is some fuel when she feels him go rigid. He sets her back on her feet but doesn't release her. He presses his nose against her neck and breaths in, smelling her just like Tiran does.

"Hey, that's not polite where I come from," Mara objects, trying to make a joke of his behavior. She tries to push him away, but Nelam's hands tighten around her. Then he draws back from her, eyes wide, mouth slack, hands tightening harshly on her upper arms. Mara watches his green skin go pale, his blue scale pattern swirling between blue and purple, as if he can't decide what emotion he's feeling.

"You smell..." he starts, then looks over to Tiran. "She smells like a..." He stops again, shaking his head. "It's not possible."

Tiran sends Nelam a warning look. "Father, please don't." He puts a hand on his father's shoulder and attempts to draw him away, but Nelam keeps his hold on her.

At this point, Mara's growing concerned. Does she smell like the enemy? Maybe Hissa don't like the smell of humans? Tiran likes her smell despite her species. Perhaps it's only his father that doesn't like her smell.

"I'm sorry if Tiran didn't warn you that I'm human," Mara starts to apologize, but before anything else can come out of her mouth, Nelam releases her shoulder and grabs the neck of her biosuit with both hands. With one violent move he rips it open, exposing her shoulder and one side of her chest halfway down her rib cage.

The assault is so unexpected that Mara's caught by surprise, and it takes precious seconds for her to react. She scrambles backward, ignoring her exposed skin, and brings her fists up, ready to defend herself if Nelam comes at her.

With a roar of anger, Tiran shoves his father away, making the man stumble into the small crowd of men, all talking rapidly to each other in Hissa as they point to her.

"Don't touch her like that," Tiran thunders at him and then looks up at the rest of the men. "No one touches her!"

All the men are staring at her with equally shocked faces. None of them are even sparing a glance at the roaring Tiran. Having her chest exposed makes her feel horribly vulnerable, but she knows better than to look down or try to pull her suit back together. Not only would that take her eyes off the threats around her, but there's probably nothing she can do. He ripped the fabric and effectively destroyed the suit.

That's the second biosuit to fall at the hands of Hissa men. She'd find that funny if the situation wasn't so dire.

She's scared. There are too many big Hissa for her to take down. Even if Tiran fights on her side, she's not sure it will end well for them. Edging back toward the shuttle, she glares at all of them, trying to hide her fear.

"Keep back," she orders, proud when her voice doesn't shake. Ignoring her, Nelam approaches, but Tiran steps in front of her, shielding her from both his father and the rest of the men.

"Sweet, wonderful woman," Nelam calls out. "Please forgive me. Please don't leave! Please accept my son into a Family Pact!" Mara's jaw drops. Out of all the things she expected to come out of Nelam's mouth, those words weren't even in the same solar system.

"What's going on?" she whispers, angry, confused, and frightened. She peeks around Tiran's bulk to see Nelam on the ground before her in supplication. He's in the same position Tiran put himself in back on her ship when he wanted to show he wasn't a threat. Nelam sits with his legs stretched out straight in front of him, hands laced behind his neck, and his head bowed. To her shock and bewilderment all the other men scramble to the ground and assume the same position.

They're deliberately making themselves vulnerable.

Strangely unperturbed by all of it, Tiran sighs and reaches down to help his father to his feet. "I haven't told her," he tells the man. "I wanted our Menders and scientists to confirm it and then tell her and offer a Family Pact. This wasn't a wise action, Father. I told you she was a slave once. Your actions could've frightened her away."

Nelam shakes his head violently. "I couldn't help myself. She smelled like your mother. So much like your mother. Like a Hissa woman. I couldn't—" He chokes on his words.

Cautiously, she comes out from behind Tiran to watch the interaction between father and son. Nelam looks at her, then drops his head in shame. "I offer my life," he tells her, "you may have me executed if you so wish for my abhorrent actions. I have no excuse."

Thoroughly shaken, Mara regards the man warily. "I don't want anybody dead. But I'd like to get out of here." She looks up to Tiran. "Can we go back to Witch now?" she pleads. He hugs her to him, gently enclosing her in his arms and drawing her into his warm embrace.

"No, my heart, we can't go back to your ship. Not any longer."

Those words make a surge of fear go through her. "I'm going back. You can stay."

His hold is still gentle but firm, and he rubs his hand up and down her back, trying to soothe her. It's not working, especially considering what he says next. "No, little warrior. Leaving right now isn't an option for you either."

Refusing to panic yet, she makes her voice firm. "You can't keep me here. I'm free."

"I need our Menders to see you," he tells her, tightening his hold when she tries to pull out of his grip.

"Let me go, Tiran," she orders, angry now. Damn them all for making her feel fear. And damn Tiran for betraying her.

He gives her a look of resignation and pleads with her. "I can't. Please don't fight me."

"You should know me better than that," she growls at him. "I don't just give in or give up."

"I know," he says simply; then she feels the pressure of a drug gun against her back. "I'm so sorry, little warrior."

Mara fights the drugs in her system, throwing a knee up and catching him in the same rib the guards cracked seven days earlier. He grunts painfully from the blow but doesn't release her. She tries again, but this time her strike is weak, uncoordinated. Her limbs are getting heavy, and she's having a hard time focusing her eyes. Tears start to stream down her face.

"How could you do this to me?" she whispers before the drugs drag her into unconsciousness.

CHAPTER

17

Mara's look of betrayal just before she succumbs to the drugs makes Tiran's heart break. He didn't want it to be like this. This wasn't the plan he'd crafted. He gathers her limp body into his arms, holding her close and rocking her gently. He knows she can't feel the comfort he's trying to give, but that doesn't stop him.

"Did she faint?" Nelam asks as he gets up from the ground. He steps cautiously closer but doesn't spare a glance at Tiran. His eyes are focused on her neck, staring greedily at the marks there.

"I was forced to use this," Tiran says as he violently throws the empty drug gun away. "Damn you to the cold depths of the Unseen Moon!" he snarls at his father. "This didn't need to happen. I wanted her to be enchanted by us, not feel threatened. Now she fears us, and her trust will be hard to win back."

Nelam blanches and takes a step away from his enraged son. "I have no excuse," he states bleakly. "I couldn't seem to help myself. I had to see her mating marks. She smells just like one of our receptive females. She smells just like your mother smelled on the day we signed our Family Pact."

"I didn't know that," Tiran admits.

"How could you? They were all dead by the time you were old enough to start distinguishing smells with any accuracy," Nelam points out grimly. "But I remember. By the moons, when did this happen?"

"The marks appeared this morning," Tiran tells him. "I wasn't sure if they were the mating marks or not. I've seen some pictures, but every female is different. I just don't know how a non-Hissa woman could have mating marks."

"Perhaps she has some Hissa in her." Mender Katim, one of the most respected Menders and researchers on Hissa steps forward. "I've been studying the Decanting technology the humans created since you sent us your update a few days ago. None of the Decanted are fully human. They all have some mixed genetics from other species. She might even have some Hissa in her. At least enough to give her some of the traits of Hissa women."

"She didn't get the size though," another male points out. "She's so tiny and delicate. Could she even carry a Hissa child to term?"

"She's rather tall for a human female," Katim informs him.

"It doesn't matter," Tiran tells them bleakly. "She's not going to want to stay." The men gasp in alarm.

Nelam touches his arm urgently. "Tell her about all the things we can give her! Tell her we are dying out!" his father pleads. "Convince her."

"I'll try," he promises. What he doesn't tell his father is that he couldn't care less about the fate of Hissa. Let them die out. Let their species cross the starry veil without progeny. He doesn't care. All that matters to him is that this woman remains in his life. If she decides to leave, he's leaving with her. There's not a future he can see without her in it, even if he has to give up Hissa. Even if he has to go against the wishes of the Council, because he knows in his heart, when the Council hears about this, they will want her to stay. And it won't matter what she wants.

Already there are men on communicators, rapidly talking to others. Spreading the news of this human woman whose skin is covered in mating marks. News will travel fast. Everyone will know soon.

What has he done?

"I'll take her to my home now. She'll be out for hours, and I have a lot of things I need to accomplish before she wakes up."

The men nod and move out of his way so he can carry Mara to the personal transport waiting for them. Mutely, they follow him, unwilling to let Mara out of their sight just yet.

"Should I come too?" Nelam asks anxiously. "I can bring my sword and death clothes. If it appeases her, she can force me to cross the starry veil." The formal words make Tiran give a humorless chuckle.

"I wouldn't do that," he warns his father. "She might take you up on it instead of just giving you a few cuts across the chest."

Nelam doesn't flinch. "I would stand still and let her cut me deep. I wouldn't struggle if she took my blade across my own throat. I would do anything to convince her, my son. Anything you need."

Touched by his father's willingness to sacrifice himself, Tiran gives Nelam a sad smile. "Leave us be for now. Let me gauge her mood when she wakes."

Nelam makes a sound of agreement as he stares at Mara's neck. "I'm at your service."

Stepping forward, Katim addresses him. "We're all at your service." A quick glance around shows that the men surrounding him all agree with Katim. "She's our first true hope, Tiran. She's a gift to us all. Unexpected and marvelous. Once the Council knows, I'm sure they'll grant anything you need to appease her."

"I'll be in touch with the Council," he promises. "Because I'm going to need their support if we're going to make her satisfied."

He has one idea that might convince Mara to stay, but it's going to take a lot of resources and perhaps the backing of the Hissa Council.

CHAPTER

18

Waking slowly, Mara knows instinctively she's not on Witch. Keeping her body still and her eyes closed, she listens intensely to the world around her and tries to figure out where she is and how she got there. She's atop something soft and warm, and the air around her smells pleasant and faintly of flowers. She's either on a very large station with an expensive bio-system, or she's planet-side.

She remembers being anxious about the trip to the planet's surface, but Tiran was so excited, and he made her excited with him. Did they make it to the planet's surface? Did she and Tiran crash as they were getting to Hissa? Or perhaps something on the planet affected her and caused a blackout. She takes a few deep breaths and smells not just flowers but vegetation also. That convinces her. She must be planet-side, not on a station.

Assessing her body for damage is the next task. Subtly she tightens and loosens her muscles limb by limb and finds no painful spots. Her skin has a familiar tightness, as if she'd been in a battle but not enough to make her think she was in a fight. Maybe the stress of forced landing put enough adrenaline in her system to make her black out?

Did they board a shuttle? Was the shuttle attacked? Her mind keeps drawing blanks, and she wants to hit her brain just like she smacks Witch's cheap control console sometimes. She hears a sound and forces her body to remain motionless.

"I not care," Tiran is speaking to someone. His accent is thick, and his Space Standard language skills are deteriorating, telling her he's agitated. "It not matter how much is cost, don't you understand? *Jamiorna suff ta neel tormalla!*"

He doesn't sound in distress. He sounds frustrated. She's pretty sure that last sentence was a curse in Hissa. If she didn't know better, she'd say he's trying to make a deal with a merchant. For a moment she thinks to end the ruse, open her eyes, and go to him. But something she hears in his voice makes her pause and wait.

Rushing into things is a good way to find yourself at a disadvantage. Waiting, assessing, and amassing knowledge are almost always the best recourse. Remaining still, she continues to listen as Tiran speaks loudly from the other room.

"Are you listening? Anything less, unacceptable." he pauses then speaks again, his voice almost yelling. "No, not any human. I give you her name and identity, only that one!"

What is he talking about? Is he trying to buy a human? Why would Tiran try and do that?

Suddenly the scene just after the shuttle landing comes back to her, and it takes every iota of control she has to remain still when her heart starts to race as images flood her mind.

Tiran's father ripping her biosuit open.

Tiran telling her she can't leave.

Tiran drugging her.

She opens her eyes just enough to take in the darkened room around her. A door opened only a few inches allows enough light in the room for her to make out shapes of things. The opening also affords her a narrow view of the room beyond. Tiran is pacing back and forth as he talks. She can't hear anyone else in the room, so he must be using a communicator. Both his movements and his voice are agitated.

"Yes, many credits, I know. I need that one human, not others, spend as needed," Tiran all but roars, making Mara flinch.

That sounds like he's buying another human. Is he buying a slave?

Years of captivity flood her mind as a small whimper escapes her. Slowly, she moves her fingers up to her throat, expecting to feel an obedience collar. When all her fingers meet is her skin, she sags with relief.

She doesn't understand the bizarre behavior of Tiran's father or the strange reaction of the other Hissa men, but one thing is crystal clear. She needs to get out of here and back on Witch. Nothing is more important than her freedom.

Careful to make as little noise as possible, she sits up and takes in the room around her. Her eyes have fully adjusted to the small amount of light filtering in through the slightly open door.

She's laying on a large round bed placed in the center of a round room. Looking down at herself, she notices her torn biosuit is gone, replaced by a loose gauzy top and matching baggy pants. Both are much too large for her and in a style she's never seen before but is similar to what she saw the Hissa men wearing when they landed. The pants have been secured with a colorful belt and when she looks closely, she can see extra holes were recently added to fit her smaller size. The clothes are comfortable, but they aren't practical. Wishing there was time to search for her biosuit, she rolls up the long sleeves of the top, thankful that at least she is clothed.

As a slave she and Lara never went naked, but she's seen enough traveling as a Cargo Hauler to know that some owners don't even allow their property the dignity of clothing. She'll take baggy garments over naked any day.

Examining the room around her more closely, she sees a few storage cabinets as well as another door that's completely closed instead of cracked open. Mara can't see anything in the dim light that would make a useful weapon, and she can't risk opening cabinets or doors, so she'll have to try and find something as she makes her way back to Witch.

Three oval windows are set high along one wall. Getting off the bed, she tiptoes over to them and finds that they're high enough that she has to make a little leap to get her fingers on the sill. Stealthily, she pulls herself up until she's perched on the sill and then pulls back the heavy drape covering the window. Outside, the night sky is brightly lit by one of Hissa's moons.

Thankfully, the window is easy to open and makes no noise. Inching herself forward, she takes a good look around. She's perched about three stories up, but there are several good-sized trees near enough to the window to be useful. She gauges the distance, takes a deep breath, and jumps.

It's close. She just barely manages to grab a branch and hold on as it bucks under her weight. Once the tree stops swinging, she works her way to the trunk hand over hand. Once there, she wraps her legs around the trunk, lets go of the branch then slides down, landing with a small thump on the wet ground.

The trip down the tree trunk shreds the soft, fragile fabric of her pants. Glad to be rid of the bulky garment, she takes them off and discards them on the ground next to the tree. The shirt is so long it reaches almost to her knees like a tunic dress. She's able to wrap the belt around it to help keep it in place.

Of course, she doesn't have shoes. Slaves don't need shoes if they aren't allowed to leave the house. If she ever gets hold of a plasma rifle or a good old hand blaster, she's going to put a few well-placed holes in Tiran's lying hide.

Intense rage rises up in her. So far, she's managed to stay relatively calm, focusing on escape instead of Tiran's betrayal. She needs to find that focus again. She can't afford to let her adrenaline spike and suffer the repercussion of helplessness afterward. She needs to keep herself composed and her energy expenditure even. She can't let herself become vulnerable while she's in such a dangerous situation.

She starts jogging along a dark path, following one of the communal tram tracks she saw from the air. She remembers they formed a kind of spoke pattern, all leading to the heart of the city where the shuttle port is located. The only thing she isn't sure of is if she's traveling toward the port or away from it. She drops to a speed she can sustain for most of the night if necessary. Pacing herself is going to be one of her most important tactics right now. Even if she does find the port, she might not make it onto a shuttle right away. She needs to have the energy to find a hiding spot if necessary. A period of reconnaissance and planning might be required, but none of that can happen if she wears herself out too soon.

After a few miles she realizes the houses are farther apart and there's more vegetation. She's going in the wrong direction. Stopping, she looks around and assesses both her surroundings and her body. She's thirsty, and her feet are starting to hurt. There's a small house nearby with dark windows. Either the occupant is asleep or not home. She hopes it's the latter because breaking into someone's home is the safest option.

Tiran mentioned to her on their way to Hissa that many houses lay empty because entire families died. The bodies were taken for ceremonial processing on one of the moons, and the houses were left alone with everything still intact. There was so much loss so quickly, the houses were left as a memory to those lost to the Great Death. If this house is one of those empty ones, her luck is getting better.

Making her way around the house, she peeks into every window looking for signs of life. She doesn't see or hear anyone, so she eases a window open and crawls inside. There's barely any light coming from the outside, forcing her to feel her way around. She needs to find something tough to tie around her feet for makeshift shoes. Something to drink would be nice too. A weapon would make her downright giddy.

A large table dominates the room with several items at one end of it. The lack of light forces her to lean very close to the table to examine the items, but she finds a stack of round rough-cut cloth, a bucket filled with something that looks like eggs, a few table knives, and several tools she's never seen before. The lack of dust tells her this dwelling is currently occupied, but as long as the occupant remains asleep, she's safe.

She tucks the knives in her belt, then ties the fabric rounds around her feet, wincing when she realizes one of her feet has a raw bloody spot on the heel. She wraps that one in an extra layer. It probably won't do much to shield her from pain, but at least she won't be leaving a trail of bloody footprints in her wake. Then she tucks a few of the items that look like eggs into her shirt. They might be good for a snack later.

Moving to the next room she sees a front door. She could go back out the window, but the door would be easier and quieter. Thirst plagues her, but she doesn't want to push her luck by exploring any further, so she decides to leave and look for water elsewhere.

She's almost out the door when the house lights up and a sleepy Hissa stumbles into the room. He's staring down at a bracelet communicator but looks up as he enters the room and sees her. They both freeze in place. He's only wearing a pair of loose trousers, sleeping pants probably. The rest of him is naked and large. The guy stands tall, with broad shoulders and chest, tapering down to a narrow, muscular waist. For the moment, he's unmoving, stunned and gaping at her. But that won't last. She needs to decide on a course of action and quickly.

Fight or flight?

She could probably take the guy, but she'd rather not try. Captain Dolan drilled into her over and over again that leaving the field of battle intact is often victory enough.

"Female," he mumbles, then sees her neck and his eyes bulge out. "Mating marks!" He stumbles toward her, galvanizing Mara into action. Running for the door, she throws it open and sprints into the thick jungle surrounding the small house.

Making a loud ruckus, the man knocks over furniture as

he scrambles after her. "Female! Please don't run away! I've got food! And wine! Please! I'm a healthy, worthy male!"

Pushing hard to gain distance from the man, she flies down the path. She knows she can't keep up this pace much longer, but at least the guy is dropping back. Unfortunately, he's not dropping back by much. Why couldn't she have broken into the house of an infirm old man?

Cursing loudly, he stumbles and falls a little more behind. She uses that advantage to push her body hard for a little more distance, making her adrenaline spike. Risking a look behind to assure he's not in her line of sight, she dives into some dense vegetation. She pulls herself into a tight ball and tries to slow her breathing. She can hear him approaching, even over the roar of her heartbeat in her ears.

"Female!" he calls out just as he gets even with her hiding spot. She expects he'll jog right past her but instead he stops, sniffing the air. She mentally curses. She'd forgotten about their excellent sense of smell.

The man moves in a small circle, smelling deeply as he goes. Now she's more worried about the sweat coating her body than her rapid breathing.

"I won't hurt you," he calls out. "I promise, no harm. Please come out. We can talk. I've got many things I'd like to show you. Beautiful clothes to dress you in. They are made of the softest fabrics." He approaches her spot, and she braces to attack.

"You're small," he calls out, taking another step toward her hiding spot. "I'm gentle. I'm known for my gentleness. I have tame Davio birds. You know they only like kind and gentle handling." He's almost on top of her. She pulls a knife out in each hand and gathers her legs under her.

Just before he might have stepped on her, he turns and starts to sniff in another direction. "My mother left many beautiful trinkets. I'd make gifts of all of them to you. Please come out, little female! I want to talk to you. Feed you. Care for you. Please!"

His pleas almost break her heart. She feels for a species with no females, so desperate for companionship and family that they are willing to make do with a worthless human. But her sympathy evaporates the moment she thinks about being owned again.

I'm free. I'm a captain. I have Witch. I will never be a slave again. I'm worth more than being someone's possession.

Still begging her to come out of hiding, his voice moves off. She stays in place until the jungle around her is quiet again. Either he's stopped calling out or he's moved far enough away that she can't hear him anymore. She hopes the authorities laugh at him when he tries to report a wandering human on the planet. If she's lucky, Tiran doesn't even know she's missing yet, and this guy's testimony will sound like the ramblings of an insane man.

Tucking the knives back into her belt, she eases out of her hiding spot, wincing when several thorns grab her skin and tear at the delicate cloth of the baggy shirt. Once free, she looks down at the shirt and cringes; it's almost more holes than fabric now. She'll be happy when she can trade the useless shirt for a sturdy biosuit. Her feet are throbbing, reminding her that a pair of boots are on her must-have list also.

Looking up at the sky, she tries to figure out what direction to travel to put her back on the path near the tram. She's never needed to navigate planet-side before and finds the stars look much different through atmosphere than a porthole in space. She can't make heads or tails of the night sky so she's just going to need to backtrack until she finds the tram line again.

Before she can start walking in any direction, she's lifted off her feet by one strong arm while the other quickly captures both her wrists.

"I'd rather not be stabbed tonight," a deep voice chuckles in her ear. She screams, kicks her legs out, and tries to bash the man's face with the back of her head. He must have known where she was hiding and pretended to give up, circled around, and waited for her to emerge.

This Hissa is a clever bastard.

"Calm, little female," the man says as he starts jogging back to the house, carrying her weight effortlessly. "Are you hungry? I have food. Let me feed you."

"Put me down!" Mara screams at him, but he doesn't even seem to hear her.

"You're lucky. I have a fresh batch of Belor fruit!" he continues cheerfully as if he's not carrying a struggling, screeching woman. He stops at his door and uses his foot to knock it open. Stepping through, he kicks it closed with his heel. "House, lockdown," he commands, and her heart drops when she hears every door and window bolt.

With the house secure, he releases the arm around her waist and drops her to the ground, but keeps her wrists shackled. "I don't think you should be playing with these," he says as he plucks out the knives she had tucked in her belt and tosses them up, so they all stick in one of the ceiling posts too high for her to reach without a ladder.

She uses his hold on her wrists to bring both legs up and kick him in the chest, but one of her make-shift shoes catches on the floor, tripping her and making the blow all but powerless. The man lets go of her wrists, picks her up and sits down at his table, cradling her in his lap and catching her wrists again before she can punch.

"Let's talk," he says with a smile. "My name's Penon. What's yours?"

Fear churns in her gut as she realizes she's going to get weak fast from adrenaline drop soon. She needs to figure a way out of this before that happens and she's completely helpless. She focuses on Penon and his eager smiling face.

"Mara," she tells him grudgingly. If it's possible, Penon's smile gets even bigger at her response.

"What are you?" he asks. He leans into her neck and smells her. "You aren't Hissa, but you smell like a Hissa female when she's found her mate and ready to have children."

"Human," Mara tells him and then thinks she might be

able to disgust him into tossing her away. "I'm a Decanted Child. Sold into slavery."

Penon's smile disappears, but he doesn't show disgust. His features turn outraged. "Who brought you here? We don't allow slavery on Hissa. I can make sure he's punished," Penon promises her. "Do you know his name? I'm glad you escaped and found me. I can keep you safe." He hugs her closer to his chest, and Mara feels a wave of fatigue wash through her. This conversation isn't going as planned.

"I have a ship," she tells him. "In orbit. I just need to get to her."

"You're a slave that owns a ship? That seems unusual," Penon says with furrowed brows. "Maybe you should start at the beginning."

"You know you can buy women, not slaves," she adds quickly before Penon can say anything more. "There are lots of women out there that would love to come here and be so," she looks for the right word, "spoiled. You say you have gifts and all that. Many women would love that. Why don't you have some of them sent? You could have your pick of hundreds of willing females."

Penon shakes his head and brings a hand up to trace the marking on her neck. "I don't know what's special about you, human, but you have mating marks. No other species we've encountered so far can do that."

"What do these mating marks mean?" Mara asks. Maybe she can convince him it's just a colorful tattoo that looks like something else.

"Back when there were Hissa women, they would find a male they liked and the two would live together for a few weeks. If they were biologically compatible, then she would show mating marks around her neck and shoulders just like you have. If the couple found they were compatible and liked each other deeply enough, they entered into a family pact."

"Biologically compatible?" Mara squeaks, not sure she wants to hear the answer.

"She can have children with the male in question. I know I didn't give you those mating marks but give me a chance to see if I can. If you don't sleep with the male who gave them to you for a few weeks, they'll disappear. Then we can see if mine will appear. Each pairing creates unique marks on the female. I understand that biological compatibility isn't everything. The female needs to know her mate is worthy. I can promise you, I'm very worthy. Whoever abandoned you to run half-naked and shoeless isn't a worthy mate."

Leaning in, he nuzzles her neck. "Please tell me who bought you and raped you. I'll have them punished. You don't have anything to fear. Everyone on Hissa will protect you. You're the first female since the Great Death to be able to mate with us. You're a prize. A gem without measure."

She'd love it if he'd stop comparing her to items someone can buy and own. Wiggling in an attempt to give herself a little personal space results in him clamping down tighter to hold her still.

"Please, don't fight," he begs. "I can smell blood on you, and I want to wash it away and check your wounds, but I'm afraid you'll hurt yourself fighting me."

Changing tactics, she goes limp and gives a little moan. "I don't feel well."

Laughing, Penon doesn't relax his hold. "Nice try, little Mara. I feel the strength in your body, and I saw how swiftly you can run. If you hadn't hid, I might never have gotten you. If you get loose, I might not be able to catch you again."

Giving up on her ruse, she sits up straight and meets his gaze. "I'm thirsty. Can I have some water?"

"Of course," Penon says, obviously delighted to provide something for her. He stands up, still holding her in his arms and walks through an open doorway. Mara realizes this is the room she was in before. With the lights on she can see it's some kind of kitchen. Penon sets her on her feet next to a counter. Thinking she can push against the counter, she braces herself. But he twirls her around and bends her over the counter before she can execute any moves. Using his superior size and weight, he pins her in place with his hip against her lower back. He grabs her hands and uses something she can't see to tie them behind her back and then release his grip. Hands bound, upper body lying on the counter, she cries out, fearful that this is the beginning of her rape.

But Penon just pats her back and makes no move to get her shirt out of his way. "Shhh, you're safe. I'm not going to violate you, sweet Mara, I just don't want you to do something rash because you're afraid." She hears him open a cabinet above her head and then the sound of water next to her. Soon, he gently lifts her upper body straight and holds a glass full of water to her lips.

She drinks deeply, uncaring of how much dribbles down her chin.

"More," is all she says when the glass is empty.

"My pleasure," Penon tells her and refills the glass from a nearby jug. She drinks the second glass more slowly and finally feels her thirst sated by the time it's empty. Penon wipes water off her face with his hands. "Feel better?"

"I'd feel a lot better if you'd let me go," Mara tells him honestly and expects Penon to laugh. He doesn't. Instead, he reaches for a small, red fruit from a nearby basket.

"Can I feed you?" he asks, begging her with his eyes. Mara gets the feeling this means something but has no idea what. Instead of violating her, he's tied her up and is trying to feed her. This has to be a first in the history of captives. Calming down, Mara starts to say she's not hungry when a loud banging startles them both.

Penon peers in the direction of his front door. "I wonder if this has something to do with you," he muses. "Why do I think I'm about to face the male that gave you those mating marks?" Mara doesn't have a clever answer for him. All she can feel is terror.

"Oh, sweet Mara, you've gone pale," Penon says, gently touching her cheek. "You have nothing to fear. I'll shield you," he promises.

The loud banging sounds again, and an enraged voice bellows, "Open!"

It's Tiran, and Mara starts to shake. Her body is exhausted with no reserves left. She's not sure she can even stand, let alone fight.

Carrying her to the door, Penon sets her down at his side, holding her up with a protective arm around her shoulders.

"Untie me," she hisses, struggling with the bindings around her wrists. They don't give at all. "I can't defend myself if I'm tied like this."

She's not surprised when he gives her a gentle look and simply says, "No."

Penon opens the door to reveal Tiran, dressed in an armored outfit and bristling with weapons. "I'm tracking a female and her scent lead me here," he tells Penon, then sees Mara. She expects him to yell at her. She waits for the rage, bracing herself as best she can, desperate to shield not only her tired body, but her broken heart as well.

Instead of doing any of those things, he drops to his knees and grabs her around the waist and buries his head between her breasts.

"I smelled blood," he says, his voice muffled against her chest. "I found your shredded pants discarded on the ground. I thought the worst. The lack of females has made some of our males violent. I thought one of them had taken you." His arms around her are so tight it's almost painful to breathe. "I tracked your smell and then started to smell blood. I thought perhaps you'd gotten loose from your abductors, but you were wounded. I thought you might be lost in the jungle, dying and alone." He makes a deep distressed sound against her, and Mara fights the urge to comfort the giant betraying bastard.

After a moment he speaks again, this time pulling his head away so he can look at Penon. "Instead of broken and bleeding, I find you safe at the home of my childhood friend."

"Did you buy her Tiran?" Penon asks, and both men

glare at each other. Tiran speaks rapidly in Hissa, stops, growls, and switches to Space Standard.

"No, never! You should know me better," Tiran berates Penon. "My little warrior bought me. She saved me from slavery. I owe her everything. She's just scared. My father didn't react well when he smelled her."

"React well?"

"He ripped her suit to see the marks," Tiran admits, shame coloring his voice.

"He attacked me," Mara protests. "Don't make it sound innocent."

"It wasn't meant to be an attack," Tiran tells her. "He was overwhelmed by your smell and acted without thought. He was desperate to see the mating marks." He addresses Penon again. "Nelam is prepared to make amends, anything Mara demands unto death."

"If you want to make amends, untie me and get me to the port," she demands, but both men ignore her. Her body is starting to get heavy, and Tiran's arms around her waist are holding her up more than restraining her now.

"Ah, that's good. Reparations will be offered. Justice and balance will be achieved," Penon states. "Those actions are highly improper, and yet I can't fault him."

When she makes a sound of outrage, he focuses back on her with a forlorn expression. "I can understand why he did it, sweet Mara. I don't approve, but I understand." He takes a deep breath in through his nose. "I want to wrap myself in your smell. I'd give you anything. If you'd picked me instead of Tiran, that is." Penon steps back, wrapping his arms around himself and violently shaking his whole body as if trying to toss something off himself.

"I'm sorry, Tiran, I know you're an honorable male. You would never hurt such a gift. If I'd known she was yours I would've contacted you. I just..." He pauses and licks his lips.

"I know," Tiran sighs. "You don't have to say it. I know the need you feel." Penon wordlessly nods his head, expression bleak.

Tiran stands and lifts Mara into his arms, cradling her to his chest. She doesn't protest. She's tired, hurt, and realizing this entire planet will just hand her right back to Tiran if she gets free again. So much for Penon's promise of protecting her.

"Thank you, Penon. You're an honorable male. We will find you a female too," Tiran tells him gently. "Mara can't be the only one of her kind out there."

"That's hope enough for now," Penon agrees as Tiran walks out with Mara in his arms.

Penon stands at his open door, the moonlight illuminating his face. Mara can see the heartbreak there as Tiran carries her away.

Yeah, she thinks to herself bitterly. *We're all heartbroken, aren't we.*

CHAPTER

19

He doesn't untie her. Even when they get back to his house. Just like Penon, he orders his house locked down the moment they're inside. Mara feels the slam of every window and door bolt like a blow to her heart.

Carrying her to his bathroom, he eases her onto a plush rug next to a large round tub. With a few taps he activates several bowls full of crystals. They light up, illuminating the room in a soft warm glow. He turns away from her to open a valve. Hot water starts pouring into the tub and steam quickly fills the room. Uncorking a bottle, he pours something viscous into the filling bath and the scent of flowers permeates the air.

She just closes her eyes and tries to ignore everything happening to her.

"I thought you stolen," Tiran tells her as he effortlessly tears the shirt off her body. To her surprise, he leaves her bra and panties on. He stares at the shirt for a moment before tossing it into a corner. "I'll have clothes custom made for you," he promises. "Everything I found was much too big, not suited to you at all. From now on, I'll make sure everything you wear will be beautiful and soft and fit just to you."

Mara doesn't respond. She lets her eyes go unfocused as she stares off into space. She needs to sleep. She needs to let her brain shut down. The physical effort of the night combined with Tiran's betrayal is just too much for her.

Big hands start exploring her body. He doesn't force her legs apart or put his mouth on her. Instead, he examines the various cuts and abrasions she collected during her escape attempt. He makes a deep sound of distress when he gets her makeshift shoes off and finds her heel a bloody mess. Retrieving several items from a nearby shelf, he tenderly cleans her wound, casting her anxious glances when she doesn't react to his ministrations. She knows it should sting, but she can't seem to feel anything right now.

It's shock, she decides. That's why she doesn't care what's happening to her. Why every sensation feels muted and far away.

Untying her hands, he cleans the long angry scratches the vines made when she came out of hiding earlier. "Our world has a lot of dangerous plant life," he tells her. "Not a lot of animals, but some of the plants can kill you if you just touch them. We don't keep the deadly ones near settlements, but when I take you hiking, I'll make sure to point them out to you."

He talking as if we are dating or married, she thinks glumly. *But then again, when you own something, you can treat it however you like.* She feels tears prick her eyes and pulls further into herself. She doesn't want to feel that. She doesn't want to feel anything.

He methodically checks every inch of her, treating every scrape, cut, and abrasion no matter how minor. He doesn't stop talking the entire time, despite her lack of response. "There's a valley I'd like to take you to. We can only take transport to the edge, and then we need to hike down into it. It's worth it though. I hiked there many times as a child. It's the last place my mother took me before she became ill."

Something in her wants to respond to Tiran's sorrow when he speaks of his mother, but she ruthlessly shuts those impulses away.

"I don't know if Penon had time to tell you anything. I'd hoped to have several days to show you all that Hissa has to offer and woo you into staying with me." Done caring for her wounds, he picks her up and eases her into the hot water. She doesn't struggle. The bath is huge and even with her legs stretched out she can't touch the other end. He props her up against the side, her chin just above the waterline.

"I never expected mating marks to appear on your skin, little warrior. I wanted you, whether we could have children or not. I sent a message to my father telling him I'd found a human. That this human is special, and I love her. I told him I intended to enter into a family pact with her even though we couldn't have children. I thought we could perhaps adopt children. Find and rescue Decanted Children before they were—" Tiran hesitates. His voice shakes when he speaks again. "Before anyone could hurt them. We could bring them here and make a family. We could keep them safe." Mara is trying to understand his words. She's exhausted. Her muddled brain is turning over slowly, making it difficult to process what he's telling her.

He stops talking and stands up. She lets her eyes focus on him and she sees nothing but pain and regret on his face. Quickly stripping out of his armor and clothes, he steps into the tub and hisses a little at the heat. She has a moment of panic as he eases his big body down behind hers. He must've felt her tense because he makes soothing sounds as he moves. "Easy, Mara. I only want to hold you."

True to his word, he settles down and wraps his arms around her. They lay there in silence for a few moments as the warm water laps at the edges of the tub.

"I was so scared you'd turn me down. Scared you would go back to Witch and leave me forever," he finally says, breaking the quiet. "I knew I needed to find something that would make you stay so I put out contracts all over the place for your sister."

She jolts at his words, and his arms tighten around her. "Contracts to locate, that's all. I thought if I could find where she is, then we could go retrieve her. Once she's here on Hissa, safe and cared for, then you wouldn't have a reason to leave me. By yourself, going from station to station you might never locate her. Even though there aren't that many humans in this area of the universe, there are many slave auctions and private owners. So many places she could be, and you have so few resources to call on." He takes a deep breath, and the tone of his voice gets lighter.

"But we have so many resources. So much wealth and so few to lavish it on. The mating marks meant it was easy to get the Council to enlist the help of the military to find your sister. I've also been given access to government credit accounts. With the wealth of Hissa behind the search, it's only a matter of time. I've already heard back from several sources. I have no doubt we'll find your sister."

Emotions overwhelm her. Wanting to see his face, she tries to turn, but he stops her motion easily by tightening his arms around her.

"You are my treasure," he continues. "When the mating marks appeared this morning, I panicked. I didn't know if I should tell you or not. I wasn't even sure if they were real. We've been looking for women that can bear our young almost my entire lifetime and haven't found any, and I decided to be content with love. And then—" He slaps the water to emphasize his point. "Mating marks appear around your beautiful neck."

The need to say something is strong, but she's buried her emotions so deep she can't seem to draw them out.

"Now all I can think about is you round with my child. I can even see her. She'll have your eyes. She'll like to run and play, and I'll be constantly picking her up because she'll fall but will refuse to give up." His words evoke an image in her mind. A girl child with Tiran's blue scale pattern on her head. She'd be tall, graceful, and half-wild. But most importantly, she'd be loved.

"I'm sorry about my father," Tiran continues. "I wanted to explain everything, and then give you all the time you wanted to decide if you would stay with me. I'd never force you." She almost makes a sound at that, considering he drugged her when she tried to leave. As if reading her mind, he sighs. "The drug was on the shuttle. I don't know what made me grab it. I didn't think I'd need it. I thought I would be able to show you Hissa, talk you into seeing the Menders. Once we knew what was going on, I'd explain and beg you to accept me."

"I know my father acted badly. But you have to understand, it's been decades with no women and no children. My father was ready to welcome you as my savior and mate, but then he caught your scent. He didn't realize what he was doing and feels a great deal of shame. I can keep him away from you forever if that's what you wish. But I hope you would find it in your heart to forgive a man presented with something precious he never expected to see."

Closing her eyes, she lets his words sink in, thawing her heart from the ice cage she erected around it.

"We all see you as a treasure," Tiran continues, and she can hear the desperation in his voice. All the emotions he's kept bottled up for so long. Desire, longing, love, and most importantly, hope.

"I love you with all my heart and want to form a family pact with you. There was never any intention to make you a slave again. I just want to be with you and make you happy." Tiran stops talking to take a shaky breath. "Because I love you more than my next breath, if you wish to leave tomorrow and never come back, I will escort you back to Witch myself."

Emotions finally break out of the deep hole she's buried them in. She wants to tell this man she loves him too and can't imagine her life without him. She wants him to know they will figure it all out together. Finding her sister, living on the planet, having kids, all of it. She wants to laugh and cry. She wants to hug him and kick his ass for not explaining everything sooner. His impulses and bad decision making are both something she can understand now because she'd do the same thing to get her sister back.

Love is one hell of a powerful motivator.

But she isn't able to say any of those things. Her tired brain is done and forces her eyes to close. The last thing she remembers is Tiran kissing the crown of her head and urging her to close her eyes and rest.

CHAPTER 20

Sensing someone hovering over her, she opens her eyes, expecting to see Tiran. When Penon's face fills her vision, she reacts instinctively, punching him in the nose with a nice powerful jab.

Rearing back with a cry of surprise, he clutches his nose and eyes her with hurt surprise. Scrambling out of the bed, she stands up to face him, fists up, ready to fight. She grins at the feeling of her rested body ready and able to do her bidding once more.

"I think you broke my nose," Penon gasps. "Why did you do that?"

"Why the hell were you so close to me?" she counters.

Thinking about that for a moment, he finally nods in agreement. "I needed to wake you but wasn't sure how to do that without causing alarm. Perhaps I should have figured out how to do it at a distance."

"You failed at the whole trying-not-to-alarm-me thing," she informs him tartly.

To her surprise, Penon gives a small chuckle and draws his hand away from his nose, which he's been feeling. It's red and quickly swelling but doesn't look broken. With a small wince, he drops his arms and regards her with a soft smile.

"I'm aware of that, and I won't ever make the same mistake again. But we really must get moving. Please come with me." He tries to grab her arm. She blocks him and delivers a nice little kick to the thigh, making Penon fall to one knee. He's no longer smiling.

"Woman, stop hitting me!" he roars out, making her laugh.

"Stop trying to touch me!" The glare he gives makes her feel much better. Finally, he's taking her seriously.

He huffs out a breath and drops his arms. "We need to get to Tiran. I'm just trying to take you to him, stubborn female."

Going pale, she drops her fists. "Is he hurt? What happened?"

"He was making arrangements to have your ship fueled when the Council had him arrested. His trial is going on right now."

"Arrested for what?" she asks, outraged.

"For buying you. No one believes that you came willingly. They all think he forced you."

Feeling incensed, she growls. "That's not correct at all! They have it all wrong! Why does no one believe *I* bought *him*?"

"I know that," Penon assures her. "But the Council doesn't understand you at all. They think you're fragile because you're so small. That's why they didn't want to involve you in the proceedings. Because they fear it might be too traumatizing for you."

"Fuck that," she grounds out. "Get me over there! I'll tell them what happened!"

Pointedly looking down, he clears his throat. "You might want to put on clothes first. For your comfort, of course, because I don't mind if you wish to stay unclothed."

Blushing, she looks down and realizes she's naked. Cursing, she stomps around Tiran's room until she finds some of his clothes. She pulls on one of his shirts. It's so long the hem hits her mid-calf. She rolls up the sleeves and digs in the closet some more. She finds some kind of soft short pants and pulls those on too. When Tiran wears them, they probably only cover him to the knees, but on Mara they go almost all the way to her ankles.

The pants are so loose they are ready to fall off, so she looks around until she spots the belt she'd worn yesterday. She cinches it around her waist and turns to face Penon. He gives her a disapproving look.

"That's an ugly outfit," he declares. "You should be wearing bright colors and soft clothes."

What is it with Hissa and clothing? She snaps her fingers a few times. "Keep focused here, Penon," she reminds him. "Tiran, on trial? Scary Council not believing him? Shouldn't we be leaving now?"

Nodding, Penon reaches for her arm but stops when she gives him a sharp look. "Apologies," he says holding up both hands palm out. "Come with me, please." He leads her out of the house and to the same kind of personal transport, similar to what she saw at the landing pad the day they arrived. He opens the door to let her in and then follows her. With a few taps on a keypad, they're moving.

Even though she's trying to be still and patient, the tension in her body makes it impossible. In an attempt to distract herself, she starts asking questions. "What's this Council anyway?"

"They're our governing body," Penon explains. "There are six High Councilors and six Lower ones and the Centrium— that's the only hereditary position. The Higher and Lower just denote the regions they were elected from. At least it used to, those regions don't exist anymore. After the Great Death, our population was so diminished that everyone moved to this city and the surrounding areas. There are only a few other places where men still live outside of here, but not many. Now Higher and Lower positions are elected by—"

"We don't have time for a civics lesson, Penon," Mara

says, interrupting him. "What I need to know is if this Council could sentence Tiran to death."

"They could, but I've never heard of a Council doing that," Penon assures her. "More likely they would assign him a job on one of our moons or a distant colony and not allow him to return to the main planet."

"Oh," she relaxes a little. "That's fine. I can just fly over with Witch and pick him up." Penon shakes his head.

"No, Mara, I'm afraid you don't understand the full implications of those mating marks. Those who saw them at the landing pad have spread the story. Not only does the Council know but most of Hissa too. This is the most significant thing that's happened to us in a long time. You represent the possible saving of our species. Our entire planet is up in arms. Some are calling for you to be housed at Medical so the Menders can oversee your health and well-being. Others are saying Tiran must care for you as a mate would. Others are demanding to meet you. No one has slept all night. We've all been in conferences with the Council. I was called in early this morning to testify. I was dismissed as they were dragging in Tiran."

"Right, so what does that mean for Tiran and me?"

"For Tiran, it means potential hard labor on Diminish. For you, I'm not sure. But if I had to guess, I would think the Council would keep you here on Hissa. They'll assume that if Tiran can make the mating marks appear, another male will be able to as well. There's no scenario I see where the Council will let you just leave," he informs her gently.

"They'd make a slave out of me?" she asks, fear spiking through her.

"No, never. We abhor slavery," Penon tells her, sounding insulted. "But they wouldn't let you leave the planet's surface. They wouldn't force a male on you, but you'd be asked to meet and talk with the best of our kind. They'd probably hold a championship to see if anyone can win your approval with feats of strength, bravery, or intelligence."

Mara didn't like the sound of any of it. "If I can't leave,

then I'm a slave."

Shrugging, he gives her a hard look. "Then let's hope you can convince the Council that Tiran is innocent because he's your best chance at leaving our planet, if that's what you wish."

Unsure how to respond to that, she remains quiet for the rest of the journey. The transport stops just outside of a massive stone structure. Clambering out, she runs up a set of stairs, only to be stopped by a pair of massive stone doors she doesn't have the brute strength to open. When Penon joins her, she pushes at him, but he doesn't even try to open them.

"Move it," she orders. "We need to get to Tiran!"

Sighing, he looks over at her. "Please try to control your temper. There haven't been women here in a long time and the Council has to think of the future of our entire race. Getting angry won't help your case."

Nodding, she pushes at him again. "Fine, I'll be calm. Open the damn doors."

With a long-suffering sigh, he puts his shoulder to one of the massive stone doors. He strains against it, grunting with the effort to open just one side. Once the gap is wide enough Mara squeezes in, ignoring Penon's cry for her to wait.

There isn't an antechamber or anything like that. The door opens right into the main meeting room and Mara finds herself faced with a large room full of Hissa men.

All conversation and activity comes to an abrupt halt as they all turn their gazes on her. Most have their mouths open in astonishment. Many are staring at her mating marks with hungry looks on their faces.

Behind her, she hears Penon finally get the door open far enough to slide in and he bumps into her back as he enters. When she stumbles forward a few steps, many hands reach out to grab and steady her. She pulls away, thankful when they release her instead of trying to grasp at her.

No one speaks as she lets her gaze sweep around the room. She straightens her back, lifts her chin, and strides to the center. The round room has seating almost all the way around, extending high up along the walls. She feels a little like she's on the stage of a theater. Off to one side stands a tall dais where twelve men are sitting separated from everyone else. She can only assume they are the Council.

A sound of distress escapes her when she sees Tiran, bruised and bound sitting on the floor in front of the dais.

"I'm so sorry, Mara," he whispers. "I didn't think they would do this." He looks over to Penon, his expression angry. "What is she doing here? You said you'd get her out. Get her safely to her ship."

"I want you safe too," Penon confesses.

When she tries to move to Tiran, several Hissa step forward to block her. "Move," she demands, and they look to the Council for instruction. None of the Council members look at the guards, instead they all stare at her.

"Are you Mara Lost, the Decanted human, and former slave?" one of the Council members asks her, ignoring her demand for the guards to move. With a sinking heart she notes that none of them look happy to see her.

"I'm all those things," she declares. "And Tiran's mine so you need to give him back to me."

"We can't do that, Mara Lost," another Council member states. "Slavery is illegal on this planet. We're overjoyed that you are here now, but we find the terms of your arrival distasteful. Tiran must be punished."

Attempting to be charming, she plasters a smile on her face. "Look, this is a big misunderstanding. I was free when I met Tiran. I'm still free. He didn't enslave me. He didn't force me." she points at the marks everyone's staring at. "I got these from mutual pleasure, not rape."

"We would like to believe you, Mara Lost, but we can't risk it. Your mind could be damaged from your captivity," one of the Council members tells her gently. "You might be too afraid to live without a master. We'll care for you here on Hissa. No one will force you to do anything against your will again. You're safe here. Some of our Menders are very good with troubled minds. They can talk to you and help you live without a master."

"You're not listening to me," she says through her teeth. "I've been free for a long time guys. I'm good on my own, honest." Several of the Council members shake their heads and look disapproving. None of them look satisfied or influenced by her statement.

"I'm sorry, Mara Lost, we can't trust you to know yourself yet. Let us care for you, and we'll give you a safe place to heal. It would be our honor to offer you the finest foods, garments, and shelter. We'll find the best of us to introduce you to. You'll want for nothing," the Council member tells her.

They aren't ready to believe her and that makes Mara all kinds of annoyed. Time to push back. Dropping the fake smile, she puts her hands on her hips and eyes the Council with a grim expression.

"If I'm free, can I just board a shuttle and leave?" Mara challenges them. She hears a wave of distressed noises rise up from the men seated and standing in the room around her.

"We're offering you everything, Mara Lost," one of the Council members who hasn't spoken yet, tells her with a shocked expression on his face. "We'll clothe you, house you, feed you. You'll want for nothing. All our men will beg you for attention. Why would you want to leave us?"

"Because the only male I want is right there," she informs them pointing to Tiran. She sees him smile at her but ignores it, keeping her focus on the stubborn Council. No wonder Tiran's communication skills are so lackluster. He belongs to a civilization of men with the equally poor ability to exchange information.

"That's the slave conditioning speaking," someone from the crowd shouts out. "Don't let her leave. She might be hurt."

Another shout, this time from a seat high on the wall. "Send Tiran away. Don't let him near her. She must be kept safe. Penon testified she ran away from Tiran. She's in fear for her future. We must make her safe."

"Quiet!" the Council member seated in the middle calls out. He turns his attention back to Mara. "This male abducted you. We have witnesses that saw you try and leave at the port. We know he drugged you and forced you to stay. We also have witnesses that say his father attacked you and tried to rape you. All of this is unacceptable. We will punish both the father and the son. You will stay here on Hissa and find another male to be worthy of a Family Pact. That is our decision."

Knowing she needs to act quickly; Mara gauges the distance to the top of the dais. She takes one running step, then leaps. She manages to make it, just barely, and the Council members all scramble forward in an attempt to grab her, probably fearful she'll fall.

She doesn't stay still long enough for them to grab her. She leaps again, this time easily grabbing the ornate chandelier hanging low in the tall building. It swings wildly for a moment, but Mara finds its momentum helps her flip herself onto the flat top of it. She takes a moment to find secure footing then looks down and lets the chandelier's movement quiet.

Hundreds of startled faces look up at her, all frozen in fear for her safety. She laughs.

"No one can enslave me," she declares. "Tiran attacked me when I bought him. I defeated him in hand-to-hand combat. I don't fear a single one of you here because I'm a skilled fighter. I left my slave identity far behind and what remains is a warrior."

"You're lying!" one of the Council members shouts, decorum falling by the wayside as she challenges their authority. "Stop this foolishness and come down."

"She is very strong and athletic, but her mind must be very compromised if she believes untrue things," someone from the audience declares. "She's much too slight to defeat a Hissa male, even a non-warrior like Tiran."

That comment shocks Mara. They don't consider Tiran a warrior? The man defeated six guards with shock sticks. What does a Hissa need to do to prove he's a warrior? Take on an entire army with both hands tied?

"Tiran trains with the warriors at the Citadel. He's just as skilled as we are," a man shouts out. "He might not be in the military, but he's one of ours anyway." Mara gives the guy a brilliant smile and watches with interest when his blue scales flush to a purple hue.

"She did almost break my nose this morning because I startled her," Penon shouts out helpfully. "She has the instincts of a fighter. I'm inclined to believe she bested Tiran."

"Mara, please come down!" Tiran begs her. "Please, little warrior, don't do this!"

"I can prove my skills!" Mara shouts out, ignoring Tiran. "I'll make a deal with the Council. Pick a champion. If I can't toss him on his back, you win. Tiran goes off to your moon, and I stay and start talking to all your lonely males."

"You can't think you'll win," declares one Council member who's been silent so far. "You're so tiny."

"Some of our women were warriors," another Council member states with an interested gleam in his eye. Voices clamor around her, all frantic and fearful for her safety.

"But she's human and fragile. We can't risk this!"

"How else will we get her down?"

"We could dart her?"

"And risk her falling when the drugs take effect?"

"We could lower the chandelier."

Mara gives a *tsk* sound and points to the rafters. "I'll just climb up into those. You guys will have a hell of a time getting me down from there."

That causes another flurry of protests and shouts. The Council leans their heads together and she watches them, anxious to find out what they'll decide. Finally, they resume their seats and quiet the room.

"You're giving us little choice," a Councilor declares harshly. "We accept your challenge, and we'll do our best not to hurt you."

Grinning, she looks down at the disgruntled Councilors.

"That's all I can ask in this situation."

The chandelier jumps a little under her, and she realizes they are lowering it. She could get down the same way she got up but decides to save her energy for the battle to come. Several large hands grab her once the chandelier is low enough, and she suffers a moment of panic, worrying that they lied to her. But the men gently place her on the ground and back away. The chandelier is raised back up, and an area in the middle of the room is cleared of chairs. Everyone gathers against the walls, looking anxious and concerned.

I guess I'm going to fight right here in the capitol building, she thinks. *I hope everyone enjoys the show.*

Rolling her shoulders to loosen up, she catches Tiran's eyes. His face is full of fear for her. Someone's gagged him, and Mara can't help but be thankful. Any words or sounds from him would only be a distraction. "Don't worry, big guy," she tells him with a smirk. "I've got this."

Then a mountain moves in front of her.

CHAPTER

21

    With a gasp, Mara takes a small involuntary step back. "This is Woken. We've chosen him as champion to battle you. Hand-to-hand, no weapons. The first one to land on their back is the loser," a Councilor declares. He glares at Mara. "Remember, you negotiated this." Then he looks to Woken. "End this quickly. Try not to do any serious damage to the female." When the crowd screams in protest, a Councilor holds up one hand and points to a corner with another. "We have Menders and equipment here. She'll be well taken care of after Woken wins."

    "Thanks for the vote of confidence, guys," Mara mutters and grins up at the giant. "Hiya, Woken. Any chance you'll just lie down for me?"

    The giant gives a rumbling laugh. "I'm sorry, small Mara," he tells her. "I can't do that. I need you to stay also. What if you pick me?"

    Mara rolls her eyes. These guys sure have a one-track mind. "Right, so how does this begin?"

    "You may strike first to begin the fight," Woken offers generously. "Please don't hurt your hand on me."

    Eyeing the giant for a moment, she considers her options. Skill, strength, and strategy. Captain Dolan drilled the importance of all three into her.

A good fighter has one of these qualities, he explained so many years ago. *A great fighter has two.*

She'd fallen right into the verbal trap and asked, *What is a fighter called when they have all three?*

He grinned and pointed to his chest. *They're called Dolan.*

She'd laughed with him at the bad joke, but the lesson was a valuable one. Fighters seldom have all three qualities and by the look of this guy, Mara hopes he's always relied on his strength and doesn't bother to train for skill or strategy.

"Brace yourself," she murmurs and launches into an attack.

There's no point to a frontal assault, so she launches herself at the dais, kicks off the side of the stone structure, and nails Woken in the side of the head with a well-aimed blow.

The giant staggers and growls. "That wasn't nice."

Dancing away from him, she looks for her next opening. "We aren't here to be nice."

He lunges for her, but she's ready for this tactic. It's how Tiran fought her the first time on Witch. The attack is slow, and she ducks away, giving him several jabs to the sternum before moving out of reach. The giant grunts from her blows but doesn't seem particularly affected.

Dodging another grab attempt, she's able to land a few more blows. The guy is slow, so she's sure she can keep out of his reach as long as she doesn't let herself get cornered. But punching him is like slamming her fists into rocks. Her knuckles are already swelling and bruising. She might be able to keep him from catching her, but she's not sure how she's going to get him on the ground.

All opponents have weaknesses, Dolan's voice echoes in her head. *Look for the weakness, then exploit it without mercy.*

He's slower than me, she thinks. *I need to use his weight against him.* She glances over at the dais, a plan forming. Her quick look is the opening he's waiting for, and he lunges for her again. She evades him by diving sideways and rolling back onto her feet in one fluid motion. The giant grabs air and straightens up, roaring with displeasure.

"I don't want to have to hit you. Let me get my arms around you and end this without injuring you. Stop moving like that so I can grab you," he demands.

That makes her laugh with genuine humor. "Does that work for all your challenges? Just demand they give up, and they do?"

Many of the Hissa in the room chuckle at her quick wit, and Woken looks thoroughly frustrated, his scales flashing brown. That gives her an idea. She needs to maneuver him to just the right spot and getting him a little more pissed would be helpful also.

"Some warrior you are," she calls out and ducks out of another attack. "How do you defeat anyone who doesn't just stand still for you?"

Almost everyone in the room gasps at her taunts, and Woken's scale pattern goes from brown to black with rage. She feels mildly guilty for the insult. The guy's been nice to her so far. He's hampered in this fight because he can't use any move that might do serious damage to her, while she's not bound by any fear of hurting him. It might be unfair, but it's the Council's fault. If these men just listened to her, none of this would be necessary. Besides, she'll apologize later.

Then an enormous fist comes barreling at her. She evades the slow punch but feels a little shocked. If she was slower, that blow might have caved in her head. Right, no apology necessary.

"Have a care!" a Council member shouts out. Woken doesn't seem to hear the warning because he punches at her again. He's good and angry now. She fends off the blows, ducking and dodging until she can feel the dais right behind her. Pretending she's trapped, she lets some fear show on her face. Woken roars and rushes at her, thinking to pin her to the solid stone dais at her back.

Mara waits, letting him almost get to her before she

launches up. Grabbing the top edge of the dais, she's able to pull herself up and roll over the lip of the stone platform, just missing Woken's charge. He impacts hard into the stone, and she's shocked when the whole dais moves a little. If she was even a nanosecond slower, she would've been suffering some broken ribs from being squished between the massive Hissa and the stone dais.

Woken's impact makes the Councilors stumble out of their chairs and move back. Crouched down, she peers over to see Woken still standing but looking dazed and staggering. A huge lump is forming on his forehead, and blood is trickling from his nose. Good to know his head isn't made of stone, even though it felt like it to her knuckles.

Gathering her body under her, she launches at the giant's back. This might work if he's dazed enough. She wraps her legs around his chest and her arms around his neck, ducking her head against him to keep her face safe and make it harder for him to grab at her. If Hissa physiology works like many other species, all his mass and muscle will make him less flexible and make it hard for him to pull her off.

Applying pressure to his massive neck, she's amazed that her arms fit around the guy. She hears him choking, and he staggers under her. Huge hands reach up to try and draw her arms off, but Mara knows that's coming and tightens her body around him, locking herself into place. He almost succeeds in tearing one of her arms off with a bruising grip when he falls to his knees, the lack of oxygen starting to finally affect him.

Her arms and legs are starting to cramp and go numb. She's not sure how much longer she can maintain her hold as he batters at her with open hands, trying to slap her off like a bug. She hears concerned voices all around her but ignores them, her entire concentration is on staying attached to the giant, determined to ride Woken to the ground.

One last blow lands on her head, and it's only training that keeps her locked around the giant's neck. She's right about his muscles limiting his mobility, which is good because if he were more flexible this strategy probably wouldn't have succeeded, and she'd be up in the rafters throwing lighting fixtures at him.

She rides him as he drops to his knees, gasping and flailing and finally falls to his stomach. She lets go of his neck and painfully pulls her legs out from under the giant. Men are reaching for her, but she slaps their hands away. Taking the Council's words literally, she uses the immense strength in her legs to roll him onto his back. The giant's eyes stay closed, but he's breathing, so she assumes he's just dazed and recovering and not more seriously hurt.

Everyone stops moving, stunned that Woken is on his back. Their astonishment gives her time to get to her feet. She's feeling a little wobbly but refuses to let that stop her. Using two different males as steppingstones, she runs across their shoulders and lands on the dais again, empty of Councilors now. Standing there, she regards all the men in the room until she finds several of the Councilors standing together.

"I win," she calls out to them. A roar sounds from the crowd. Some are joyful at her bravery and victory. Others are enraged by the outcome. When the sound dies down, the Council steps forward, all forced to look up at her now. It's a nice reversal of positions.

"Yes, Mara Lost," one of them tells her with a sad, bitter smile. "You've won and proven your strength and skill. We believe you now. Tiran hasn't warped your mind or forced your will. We'll honor our bargain." He turns to issue an order. "Release Tiran, and free Nelam from the holding cell."

Unsure whether she should come down from the dais or not, she searches the crowd for a familiar face. When she sees Tiran standing on the ground just under her, she sags in relief.

He opens his arms, and she doesn't even hesitate. She leaps to him. He catches her easily and hugs her tightly. Wrapping her arms around him, she kisses him. After a moment, he pulls away a little so he can see her face and winces. Her face feels hot and swollen, so she knows some of Woken's strikes did damage.

"You don't look so great yourself," Mara teases him.

"Let's go home and get cleaned up," he tells her and starts walking. "Then we'll go get your sister."

Gasping, she grabs his face. "You found her?"

"Yes, little warrior, I received news this morning. It was confirmed by two independent sources." She releases his face and wraps her arms around him in a fierce hug, tears streaming from her eyes.

"You found her!"

"Of course, I did," Tiran admonishes her with a small smile. "I'd move planets to see you happy. Finding one female is hardly that much of an effort."

Woken, Penon, and several of the Councilors watch Tiran stride out, tenderly carrying Mara in his arms. Every single male wishes they could trade places with him.

"She's astounding," Woken murmurs, voice and expression full of admiration. "I can't fault her skills. She could teach some of us about movement and evasion. Trying to get my hands on her was like trying to catch water." Then he gives a small sound of disgust. "I've been warned I need to learn to be calm during battle. I let my anger control me."

"Indeed," Councilor Damir says with a frustrated expression. "And I should've picked a smaller, faster warrior."

"I'm fearful that we've lost her now," Councilor Marum sighs.

"No," Penon disagrees. "They'll find her sister and Tiran will talk them both into coming back here."

"There's a sister?" Woken asks with eager interest, making Penon chuckle.

"Yes, she has a sister," Penon repeats and finds all the men around him staring at him, renewed hope on their faces.

Penon shrugs and shares more good news. "And there were many women like the sisters produced and sold. I found a few records, and their line of children was very popular for a while. If we look hard, we might find many more like Mara."

Woken slaps Penon on the back, almost knocking the smaller male to the floor. "That's excellent news," he cheers; then suddenly his smile disappears, replaced by an expression of consternation. "I must prepare my house and grounds. I haven't tended to the Nooe bushes in years. I must try to get them to flower. The smell will please a female. And I need to order new bedding and clothes. She'll want clothes. There is much to do before they get here." With those words, he hurries off, and Penon watches as most of the men file out of the building, echoing similar things. They're all eager to make their own homes as appealing to a potential mate as possible.

They are all smiling, laughing, and moving with purpose.

For the first time in a long time, there is real hope for the future of the Hissa.

CHAPTER

22

Several weeks later and far from Hissa-controlled space

A blaring klaxon sounds through the ship, making a bolt of fear go through Lara Stray. She rushes down a narrow gangplank, and when the ship shudders violently, she almost falls into the common area below. Moving as fast as she can, she makes it to the small alcove she uses for a room. Once there, she opens the hatch in the floor and drops down onto the bridge, startling the pilot, Deena Clanless, co-owner of their small cargo ship. Deena gives her a sour look and then turns her attention to the bucking ship.

Looking at the displays, Lara tries to figure out what threat is setting off the warning klaxon. "What's going on?"

"We're under attack," Deena says with a grim expression. "Raiders. They've already disabled one engine, but I'm pushing as hard as I can with the other three."

Without hesitation, Lara moves to jump back up and leave the way she arrived. "I'll go back and see if I can get you any more out of the remaining engines," she calls out as she disappears up into the alcove. Her path is cramped but direct and soon she drops down into the engine room to the sound of numerous alarms going off. She checks the displays and finds another engine is down.

Pulling off a couple of wall panels, she climbs into the cramped confines of the engine and starts pulling wires. Their only hope is for her to disable the engine safeties so they can burn hotter and try to outrun the raiders.

Grabbing wires, she brutally rips them out, ignoring the pang of pain she feels at being so destructive to the engines she's nurtured and cared for over the years. She pulls out her com and taps it. "Go for full-burn." She's forced to scream so she can be heard over the roaring of the two remaining engines.

"How long can we do that?"

"Maybe ten minutes," Lara responds. "Then if we don't shut down, the engines will overheat and explode."

"Better that than being caught by raiders," Deena responds with brutal honesty, and Lara has to agree. She was rescued from a raider captain years ago and still carries the scars of her experience. She vows she'll never let another one touch her again.

The sound and vibration from the engines pushed to their very limit forces Lara to crawl out and flee the engine area entirely.

There's little hope they'll be able to outrun the raiders. There aren't any ports, docks, or settlements within a ten-minute flight, even at full-burn. Their only hope is the raider will burn out their engines before catching them. It's an unlikely scenario but better than just giving up and letting them capture the ship. Determined to live her last moments of life bravely, she makes her way back to the bridge. If she's going to die, she wants it to happen standing next to her friend.

Smoke starts pouring out of the engines and follows Lara back as she drops down onto the bridge again. She hurries to Deena's side, hugging the woman, and starts to cry. "I'm sorry," she says, and Deena releases the controls and hugs her back. So much for being brave.

"We had a good run," Deena tells her. "I'm sorry we never found Mara."

Trying to control her sobs, she hugs her friend tighter. "Thank you for finding me."

"Hey," Deena tells her as she draws back. "Thanks for being the best mechanic in the sector and the most loyal friend I've ever had."

Black smoke swirls around the room and both look up to the hatch Lara left open. "I guess it won't be long now," she murmurs.

"Yeah," Deena sighs. "If we could've just . . ." whatever she was about to say is cut off when the ship's coms come to life.

"Ship Ally! I'm calling to the ship designation name: Ally! Respond! This is Hissa command ship Steadfast"

Deena lunges for the control console to respond, "This is Ally. We could use some help right now." Lara wonders what a Hissa ship is doing so far from home but doesn't say anything. She's too full of hope for rescue to ask any questions.

"Throttle back your engines, we can see on our display you're about to overheat them. Throttle back now."

Jabbing at several controls, Deena initiates emergency shut down procedures, and the ship stops shuddering around them. Unfortunately, black smoke is still filling the small interior of the bridge. Lara runs to grab a couple of breathing masks and thrusts one at Deena.

"We've cut the engines. Warning, there are raiders behind us, repeat, raiders behind us."

"Acknowledged, we've already engaged the raiders with several of our ships. We read your ship as highly unstable, prepare for an emergency boarding."

"Damn," Deena mutters darkly. An emergency boarding would mean they're going to attach one of their specialty shuttles to her ship and punch holes in her hull. The Ally would be junk once that happens, her hull integrity shattered. Deena pats the control console, saying goodbye to the ship that had sheltered the two women for so long.

Lara feels bad for Deena. The ship's value wasn't just as property but as a symbol of her freedom. Ally meant the world to both of them, and soon it would be nothing but space junk. Lara huddles next to Deena's chair, not sure what to do but hoping the Hissa arrive before the air supply in their masks runs out.

Something strikes the ship, and they can hear a mechanical grinding sound. Crystal tipped drills appear, then cutters. Finally, a large piece of the hull is hauled out of the way by a massive man and tossed behind him. He steps onto their bridge, coughing from the smoke and peering around. Lara stands and raises a hand to greet him, but when the big man sees her, he launches his bulk toward her.

Fearfully, she flinches away, but the man doesn't hit her. Instead, he picks her up and effortlessly tosses her over his shoulder. Lara's mask is knocked off, and she starts coughing violently. She feels herself moving, and then more hands are grabbing her, and she realizes she's being passed through the opening they made in Ally.

The hands sit her in a chair and push another mask onto her face. She's still coughing, but it isn't as bad. As long as she keeps her eyes closed, she can keep most of her fear at bay. She can hear voices all around her but keeps her concentration on breathing.

Then Deena is put in the chair next to her, gasping and coughing also. She grabs the woman in a death grip, and even though Deena doesn't like to be touched, she doesn't struggle out of Lara's hold.

The shuttle hatch closes, and Lara hears a voice yell, "There were only these two. Hatch is secured. It's safe to leave."

The shuttle vibrates for a moment, then separates from Ally. Lara feels fresh tears prick her eyes. They've lost Ally. They lost their ship. Sure, it might have been a broken-down piece of shit that demanded every bit of her attention and skill to keep it running, but it had been their own. It belonged to them, and now they had nothing.

No, Lara corrected herself. They still had each other.

And if they're alive, they will eventually figure out how to start searching for Mara again. That's more important than anything else.

Looking around, she watches massive men moving around them in the small shuttle. This is the first time Lara's seen a Hissa in person, and she's intimidated by their size. One of the big men kneels in front of her and gently touches her knee. She shrinks back and whimpers.

"Easy," he says, holding up his hands to show he won't touch her again. "I just need to check you for injury. If you can talk to me, I don't need to touch you."

"She's scared of men. Do you have any women on board to check her?" Deena asks, drawing Lara closer to her. The giant frowns and nods.

"Yes, we have one female aboard the main ship. We are going there now. Please try and keep her calm."

"If all you guys will just keep your distance, that'll make keeping her calm easier," Deena tells him bluntly.

"Understood," the man says, then turns to the others and calls out for everyone to move to the front of the ship. He tells them that the women will disembark first and once they're down the hall the rest of the men will follow. Lara keeps her eyes closed tight but feels intense relief at the giant species' willingness to give the two of them all the space they can. But even knowing they're going to stay away, she still feels trapped on this tiny shuttle, helpless in the face of so many large males.

The familiar panic wells up.

"Breathe," Deena whispers to her. "Just keep breathing. Fear is just an emotion. Don't let it be more important than it is."

Concentrating on Deena's soft, comforting words, she brings up wiring schematics in her head to distract her. By the time the shuttle is docking with the Hissa command ship, the panic is starting to subside enough to allow her to release Deena and stand on her own two shaky legs.

The shuttle crew must have warned the main ship about her fears because all the men on board keep a respectable distance from her as she walks through the hatch to the main ship. The place is a bustle with activity, and she hopes they'll at least let Deena and her share a cabin for a while before they drop them off. She desperately needs to sleep off the aftereffects of the adrenaline. She knows Deena will be there to guard her back.

"Lara?" The familiar voice makes Lara lose her footing. Looking up, she stumbles right into Deena.

"Hey, watch it!" Deena grumbles, gaining her balance and helping Lara stay on her feet. Lara isn't paying any attention to her captain and friend; she can't take her eyes off the woman in front of her.

Looking up to see what Lara's staring at, Deena sucks in a sharp breath. "It's you. That woman looks just like you."

The woman in front of them is almost identical to Lara except she is a little leaner, more muscled, and with long luxurious hair. And she stands with confidence, shoulders back and head held high.

"Mara?" Lara asks taking a hesitant step forward. Mara sprints and they embrace in a tangle of limbs, crying and laughing.

"You're safe," Mara whispers in her ear. "We're safe. No one will ever hurt us again."

Clinging to her sister, Lara can't believe they're together again. She's thought about this day so much over the years, always hopeful, but never actually believing it would happen.

"I have a home for us," Mara tells her. "I'm going to take you there."

"Home?" Lara manages to say around the tears.

"Home," Mara confirms, and Lara knows she's truly safe at last.

CHAPTER 23

Gently closing the door, Mara gives Tiran an anxious look. "She's finally calm, but that was a bad panic attack. What happened?"

Sighing, Tiran pulls her into his arms, "Deena wanted to see the power plant just outside the city zone, and Lara wanted to go with her."

Seeking out comfort, she nuzzles Tiran's neck, right over the tattoos he received as part of their family pact ceremony. They are an exact match to her mating marks except his tattoos are black while her marks are red. She loves these tattoos, a visible reminder of Tiran's dedication to her. Not that his love for her is ever in doubt, but her eyes always seek them out, physical evidence of his commitment.

"That's safe," Mara said with a frown. "No one should have bothered them. Their escort would've dissuaded everyone. Hell, Woken's a damn mountain. Between him and Penon, no one should've gotten close enough to scare her. Were they mobbed?"

"Penon got called away on an emergency. A man got badly hurt deep in the jungle, and Penon is our best tracker. Woken was left guarding both of them alone until the replacement arrived. Lara wanted to see the engine very badly so Woken let her."

"Why didn't he go with her?" Mara asks with angry censure. "From what I know of Deena, she can fend for herself. Lara's the vulnerable one."

Despite his worry, Tiran gives her an amused look. "There's not much room in that area of the plant. It would be a tight fit for me, Woken would've immediately gotten stuck."

Chuckling, she pictures Woken stuck in a small corridor. "Right, I can see that. Then what happened?

"Two males were working up there that Woken didn't know about, and they saw Lara and rushed to her. They wouldn't have done anything. They just wanted to meet her and invite her to their homes, but she panicked. She ran from them and then tried to crawl into a duct that goes past an area too hot for a human to survive. One of them was afraid she'd get hurt so he grabbed her ankle and pulled her out."

"Oh," Mara's eyes darkened with sadness. "And I guess that's when she went into full panic mode."

Hugging her tightly, Tiran nods. "Your sister's fragile."

"Life was way worse for her after we were parted," Mara whispers. "She's only told me bits and pieces so far, but I have a bad feeling she was seriously abused for a while. I failed her," she states miserably.

"No, you didn't," He growls out. "You found her and brought her here."

"I'm not sure that's going to be much help," Mara points out. "I brought a woman scared to death of men to a planet where there is nothing but men."

"No, my little warrior. You brought your sister to a place where she will be cared for and safe for the rest of her life. After today, I asked the Council if they could make an announcement about your sister. Everyone will be informed of her fears and will keep a safe distance. They're bringing one of our best Mind Menders from the mining colony on the second moon. Our Body Menders heal physical wounds, but he specializes in helping those whose minds aren't working right. He'll be able to help her."

"I hope so," Mara says and snuggles into Tiran. "It hurts me to see her this way."

Picking her up, he cradles her against his chest. "Give her time my warrior. Wounds this deep can't be healed in a few days. We've waited decades for women as special as you and your sister. We know how to be patient. Follow our example. Lara will heal. I think she's stronger than you realize."

He carries her to the bedroom and nudges the door almost closed behind him. Because he knows Mara will want to be able to hear Lara if she wakes and needs her, they never close doors all the way anymore. Deena has walked in on them naked several times, and Tiran smiles at the memory of the pilot's appreciative appraisal when she examined his body. Mara hadn't appreciated it at all, and after a little name calling and shouting, Deena retreated, promising to be more careful.

Although she smirked the entire time she promised.

Hopefully, Lara will be stable enough to move both her and Deena to separate housing soon. At best Deena is a trial. At worst she seems to enjoy deliberately causing discord. But Lara won't be parted from her, which means that for now all four of them live in his house.

At least the weekly trips on Witch seem to be helping Lara cope. She's already delved deep into Witch's engines, mumbling about poor maintenance, and cooing to the ship that she's going to "fix her up right." Witch seemed to have formed a bond with Lara almost as strong as the one she has with Mara. Trips around the Hissa system help all three bond, and Lara never fails to come back with a big smile on her face.

They're scheduled for another trip on Witch tomorrow. He's going to see about setting a schedule to make the flights more frequent, at least while Lara is struggling so much. He's sure Mara will appreciate more time with her beloved living ship also. He should broach the subject of perhaps converting Witch's cargo hold into large living quarters so they can spend more time on her in comfort instead of crammed in the cabin or freezing in the cargo hold.

Dismissing those plans for now, he settles Mara on the bed and then lays down next to her. Drawing her body close, a familiar peacefulness spreads over him as she relaxes. She absently runs her hands over the tattoos around his neck. When Mara agreed to enter a family pact with him, an exact copy of her mating marks was tattooed on his neck and shoulders as is tradition. Mara winced as he was tattooed, but he couldn't have cared less about the ancient and painful tattoo process. The only thing he felt was the deep satisfaction of bearing matching marks to the woman he loves so deeply.

Other men stared at him now, gazing at the tattoos with envy and longing. Every time he catches someone looking at them, he realizes how very lucky he was to be captured and sold as a slave.

"Thank you for entering a family pact with me," he whispers, running his fingers along her mating marks. "You know, these mean we could have children, if you aren't pregnant already. Everyone is hopeful you'll be round with child soon.

Mara stiffens in his embrace. "I have an implant to control my cycle. It can be erratic. The implant keeps my body regular, but it also keeps me from getting pregnant."

"Our Menders can remove it if you like. I know they're doing a great deal of research about humans and Decanted Children." Her tension doesn't ease, and Tiran strokes his hand down her side, waiting patiently. There's something his little warrior needs to tell him.

Finally, Mara takes a deep breath, and the words rush out of her. "I'm scared to have children. I'm scared to be a mother."

"You'll be an exceptional mother," Tiran assures her.

"I never had a mother. Lara and I were grown at an accelerated rate in the vat so in half a year we were the biological age of a six-year-old, with the mental capacity of a teenager, and the language skills of a well-educated adult already genetically programmed in our minds. They call it unpacking when they put us through the specialty learning courses so that within another six months, we had the base knowledge needed to be the kind of slaves the family who bought us wanted. There was one woman, one of the teachers. She was kind to us and would hug us, but other than that it was just the two of us. I never learned how to be a mother. Real children are fragile. I might not be fit to raise them."

The hitch in her voice tears at his heart, and he hugs her tightly to him. "Your instincts are to protect and nurture. Look at how you treated me when I was helpless. You nursed Witch back to health. Look at how much you do for your sister. I was there last night when you held her through her nightmare. I have faith in you, little warrior. Please have faith in yourself." They lie there in silence as she digests his words. Finally, her body starts to relax again.

"I guess I've got you for back up, to help me figure it out. You had a mother for a while. You remember her. You can just tell me what she did."

"Then all you need to do is hold them, laugh with them, and protect them. That's what I remember about my mother."

"I think I can do that. Maybe we can go over to medical tomorrow and talk to one of the Menders about removing my implant."

Running his hands up her chest, he cups one of her breasts in his palm. "Should we practice so we're ready when your implant is removed? I wouldn't want to disappoint you in any way."

"As if you could." Mara chuckles at his teasing. She shivers and moves against him as his fingers grasp her nipple just the way she likes it. "I love you with all my heart."

"I love you, mind, body, and soul, little warrior." Tiran nuzzles her neck and knows she can feel his cock getting hard against her back.

"I can't imagine my life without you," she admits as she gets her hand between them and grasps his hardening flesh in her strong capable fingers.

"Luckily for you," Tiran tells her while she moans. "You never have to."

Dear Readers,

Thank you for reading *Buying Tiran*. If you want more Hissa Warriors the next book, *Tempting Selon*, is available.

I hope you enjoyed *Buying Tiran* enough to leave a review! As an indie writer without the support of a publishing company, I need all the help I can get. Your good reviews keep me writing.

If you have any questions, comments, or suggestions feel free to contact me via email: Author@RK-Munin.com

Check out my website:

www.RK-Munin.com

You can find all kinds of links there including free novellas!

Cheers,
Rye

OTHER BOOKS BY RK MUNIN

-Science Fiction-

Hissa Warrior Series
Rescuing Halin (Mian and Halin)
Buying Tiran (Mara and Tiran)
Tempting Selon (Lara and Selon)
Defying Kilan (Deena and Kilan)
Healing Mavito (Raleen and Mavito)
Claiming Yopin (Mouse and Yopin)
Teasing Woken (Safena and Woken)
Defending Revin (Kamaril and Revin) – Coming soon
Trusting Warik – Coming soon
Evading Miran – Coming soon

Human Pets of Talin Series
Loving Captivity (Sora and Searin)
Escaping Captivity (Lakin and Dalt)
Negotiating Captivity (Nalia and Derani)
Fighting Captivity (Zia and Palforma)
Tender Captivity (Jinna and Holian - This is a novella you can get for free
by signing up for my newsletter)
Craving Captivity (Lasha and Tamerin)
The Twelve Nights of Halloheen: A holiday mashup novella (Isla and
Tisuran)
Stealing Captivity – Coming soon

Origins
(A Human Pets of Talin Series)
Creating Captivity (Ari and Bazium)
Gossamer Chains (Rain and Hesarium)
Golden Cages – Coming soon

-Paranormal /Urban Fantasy-

Ours Evermore Series
Two Wolves for Soren (Soren, Kalli, and Quinn)
A Hacker, Vampire, and Chimera Walk into a Bar….(Tobias, Briar, and
Memphis)
When Darkness Meets Dawn (Imani, Lex, and Mac)
Tag, You're It (Short Story)
Kidnapping Their Third (Cora, Pike, and Kimble) – Coming soon
Pastries on a Plate and Blood in a Mug – Coming soon

Alpha Series

Alpha Mage (Emma and Kade)
His Alpha Mage (Avery and Jason – Novella)
Alpha King (Cathleen and Lazlo)

New Clan Series
Stray Wolf (Steph and Eli)
Lost Lion (Maeve and Cyrus)
Reluctant Cervid (Tavi and Donovan)
Broken Thorn (Sabina and Theodosius)